MW00639887

THE CLARION AWARDS

THE
CLARION AWARDS

Edited by Damon Knight

DOUBLEDAY & COMPANY, INC.
GARDEN CITY, NEW YORK
1984

All of the characters in this book are fictitious,
and any resemblance to actual persons,
living or dead, with the exception of
historical personages, is purely coincidental.

Library of Congress Cataloging in Publication Data
Main entry under title:

The Clarion Awards.

1. Science fiction, American. I. Knight, Damon, 1922–
PS648.S3C54   1984   813'.0876'08

Introduction copyright © 1984 by Damon Knight.
"The Etheric Transmitter" copyright © 1984 by
Lucius Shepard.
"Beast and Beauty" copyright © 1984 by Kristi Olesen.
"Lost Lives" copyright © 1984 by Nina Kiriki Hoffman.
"Flawless Execution" copyright © 1984 by Dean Wesley Smith.
"Geometry" copyright © 1984 by Jan Herschel.
"One Last Hunting Pack" copyright © 1984 by Patricia Linehan.
"The Coming of the Goonga" copyright © 1984 by Gary W. Shockley.
"Fugue" copyright © 1984 by William Knuttel.
"Up Above the World So High" copyright © 1984 by
Mario Milosevic.
"Snows of Yesteryear" copyright © 1984 by Barbara Rausch.
"The Cottage in Winter" copyright © 1984 by McNevin Hayes.
"Loaded Dice" copyright © 1984 by Rena Leith.
"Vines" copyright © 1984 by Lois Wickstrom.
"Pursuit of Excellence" copyright © 1984 by Rena Yount.

ISBN: 0-385-18383-6
Library of Congress Catalog Card Number 82-46030
Copyright © 1984 by DAMON KNIGHT
All Rights Reserved
Printed in the United States of America

First Edition

*This book is dedicated, with affection and gratitude,
to R. Glenn Wright, Leonard N. Isaacs and Herman King
(all of Michigan State University),
who kept Clarion alive.*

THE CLARION AWARDS, 1984,
are presented jointly by
Doubleday & Company and Michigan State University:

First prize: $200
"The Etheric Transmitter" by Lucius Shepard

Second prize: $150
"The Coming of the Goonga" by Gary W. Shockley

Third prize: $100
"Pursuit of Excellence" by Rena Yount

The judges are:

ALGIS BUDRYS

MARTA RANDALL

ORSON SCOTT CARD

KATE WILHELM

For Doubleday & Company, Inc.

PAT LOBRUTTO

TERRENCE RAFFERTY

CONTENTS

INTRODUCTION

One of the best things I ever did in my life was to organize the Milford Science Fiction Writers' Conference, with Judith Merril, in 1956. Judy and I were both living at that time in Milford, Pennsylvania (winter population about a thousand); Jim Blish, who with his wife Virginia Kidd had discovered Milford and attracted the rest of us, was living in New York then.

Neither Judy nor I had ever been to a writers' conference; we were naïve enough to take the words literally, and we sat our writers down in a circle, with no chiefs or Indians. That was the beginning.

In 1967 Robin Scott Wilson, who had published several stories in *Analog* (as Robin Scott), asked to be invited to the conference. He told us that he was ex-CIA, now an English teacher at a small Pennsylvania college. He arrived and turned out to be a muscular man who wore skivvies and had his hair cut very short. We became a little nervous when we discovered that every time we looked over our shoulders, Robin was there, listening. On the last day of the conference, he told us what he was up to: he planned to start a summer s.f. writing workshop at Clarion College, in Clarion, Pennsylvania, and he had come to Milford to see how we did it and pick his instructors.

Robin's inspiration was to combine the Milford workshop method with a little lecturing for aspiring writers (Milford was for professionals). From the beginning, it worked. Among the students that first year were Vonda N. McIntyre and Ed Bryant.

After two years at Clarion, Robin moved on to a succession of more glamorous jobs (he is now president of Chico State College in Chico, California). He continued to teach the first week of the workshop, but he was no longer able to direct the whole program. The workshop survived a tottery year at Tulane in New Orleans and then found a permanent home at Michigan State University in East Lansing, Michigan.

Every year, twenty applicants are invited to come to the workshop for six weeks. They live in the dorm, eat cafeteria food, swelter in the Michigan summer. Each week they have a different instructor, except for the last two, when Kate Wilhelm and I teach together. As at Milford, we sit in a circle and take turns in criticizing each manuscript. It is understood that the criticism must be (a) technical, and (b) honest. By subjecting each other to this kind of examination, the students learn to become critical of their own work.

They don't get much sleep. They write all night, shamble into the workshop room in the morning. They form intense personal relationships. Many of them stay in touch with each other, and with us. I won't say it is impossible not to love them, but I will say it is *difficult.*

The academic sponsors—MSU professors who organize the workshop in rotation (nobody except Glenn Wright can stand to do it two years in a row)—run interference with the campus police, the housing directors, etc., sit in on the workshops, solve personal problems and hand out Kleenexes. They have often told us how much they envy us. Clarion students are there because they want to be; they are handpicked and highly motivated; they work hard.

Some people who come to Clarion find out they can't become professional writers; others find out that, for one reason or another, they don't want to be. We are taking a risk with every new student, but if we knew in advance which ones would succeed, there would be no challenge and the enterprise would fall apart because it would be boring; if we *thought* we knew, we would not work as hard as we do to help the stragglers.

In the early years we had a large proportion of people who were there because Clarion was a writing workshop, not because it was about science fiction, and the first Clarion anthology reflects that. Nowadays all the students are interested in writing s.f.

and fantasy, although we let them write anything they like,* and a number of mainstream stories still get workshopped.

One thing I have noticed is that the students seem to know more every year. There are things we no longer have to teach, exercises we no longer use. I have a feeling that knowledge diffuses somehow, maybe by pheromones drifting invisibly across the continent.

The Milford-Clarion idea has diffused, too. There is a yearly workshop at Milford-on-Sea, England, founded by Jim and Judy Blish. There is a Dutch workshop, and there are or have been local workshops run by Clarionites in Chicago, Los Angeles, and Turkey City, Texas.

This anthology and the awards and the jury were all the idea of Al Sarrantonio, formerly Pat LoBrutto's assistant at Doubleday and, not coincidentally, a Clarion graduate. It was also Al's idea that the anthology should be open to all Clarion graduates from the years 1976 to 1982 who had not yet published any fiction in a professional periodical or book. That would give a chance to everyone who came along after the last Clarion anthology was put together *(Clarion,* edited by Kate Wilhelm, Berkley, 1977).

I took all this as a package, but then I had to interpret the rules, which I did by saying arbitrarily that all Clarionites from those years were eligible who had not published fiction professionally *as of the date of my announcement letter.* Accordingly, some of the writers represented here had had stories accepted but not published before my announcement, and some have in fact been published at the time I write this.

Another part of our agreement, which Doubleday accepted gracefully, was that I would have a free hand in choosing the stories, and that in order to give a fair picture of the work done at Clarion, I would include a few stories that are neither science fiction nor fantasy.

---

* Any kind of short fiction, that is. We can't handle articles or poetry, and we discourage people who want to bring pieces of novels to the workshop: it is too frustrating to try to criticize something whose form cannot be seen because it is unfinished.

There are two kinds of anthologies of short fiction, and the motives for doing them are different. An anthology of reprinted stories is an effort at preservation. Once a story is in print in an anthology, it has a chance of escaping the silence that descends over stories in magazines. In hard covers, it may last for years in libraries; other anthologists may pick it up.

An anthology of original stories, particularly one that publishes unknown writers, is an effort to bring something into being. My *Orbit* anthologies (twenty-one volumes, 1966–80) are of this kind, and so is this book. In the past I have had the pleasure of introducing such writers as Gene Wolfe, Vonda N. McIntyre, Gardner R. Dozois, Joan D. Vinge, George Alec Effinger, Jack Dann, Charles L. Grant, and Kim Stanley Robinson. It will be interesting to look at this book ten years from now and see how many of its fourteen writers are no longer unknown.

Damon Knight
Eugene, Oregon
May 28, 1983

THE CLARION AWARDS

Any person who, like myself, has survived from the Dark Ages of science fiction will recognize in this story the lamplit extravagance of late-nineteenth-century and early-twentieth-century drawings and engravings—the forest of metal rods tipped with crystals, the mysterious underground lake, the winged monster, the iron cage. If you have never met these images before, never mind; the text is its own superb illustration.

FIRST PRIZE

THE ETHERIC TRANSMITTER

BY LUCIUS SHEPARD

At 1:27 P.M. on July 19, 1985, a muggy summer's day idling the streets of Paris, diners in Brebant's restaurant atop the third platform of the Eiffel Tower were startled by a woman's agitated voice issuing, apparently, from midair.

"People of France! I must tell you of terrible outrages . . . crimes! I am speaking from the year 1905, from a cavern beneath the home of the Comte de Beaumanoir in Quercy. The device which permits me to speak is an etheric transmitter and is, in itself, the reason for my communication—"

The voice broke off with a gasp, and for nearly half a minute thereafter labored breathing was heard, as well as a hiss which swelled in volume, emanating not only from Brebant's but—as if it were an infection spreading along the iron girders—from every part of the tower. When next the voice spoke it boomed out over the Champ de Mars, distinct for a range of several hundred yards and audible as a murmur at points along the Quai d'Orsay and the boulevard des Invalides.

"I have suffered injuries to my ribs which make prolonged speaking arduous. I must repair myself as best I can. . . . *Pardon.*"

Security guards cleared the tower and searched unsuccessfully for a recording device, for explosives; the voice's initial statement had smacked of treasonous intent and a right-wing group was suspected. The afternoon edition of *L'Express,* however, reported the incident as a hoax, and a radio journalist suggested that the voice might be the spirit of Paris itself objecting to Brebant's faltering cuisine.

A crowd estimated at eight to ten thousand gathered beneath the piers of the tower. Their mood was festive, in keeping with the golden summer evening, and as the tower's intricate shadow blurred and lengthened, they shared bottles of wine and sang. Vendors sold balloons and ices and souvenirs; lovers kissed; reporters armed with tape recorders sought out those who had heard the first transmission; bicyclists in bright plastic helmets patrolled the perimeter. Beneath one of the Seine-side piers a pretty ballet student performed a solo passage from *Le Sacre du Printemps* while onlookers applauded and called out playful obscenities, sentiments she appeared to appreciate equally. A clerkish-looking man wearing a cheap brown suit proclaimed the day of Armageddon and preached a gospel of humility and repentance, but he was shouted down.

At five minutes past eight there came a rustling sound from the tower, overriding the hiss, as if enormous pieces of paper were being shuffled. The crowd grew murmurous and then the voice boomed out once again, causing the more sensitive among them to cover their ears and driving others back in momentary alarm.

It seems so foolish to be speaking to the air and expecting a result (said the voice, melancholy). I wonder to whom I *am* speaking, to what age . . . whether the chestnuts are in bloom along the rue du Faubourg-St.-Honoré or whether it is snowing. . . . Oh, what I would give for a glimpse of that sooty Paris snow which I used to rail against. I cannot read the settings of the transmitter, they are marked in the Count's private notation. But the red dial is jammed a millimeter forward into the future. How much time, I wonder, does a millimeter represent? Ah, well . . .

A deep, indrawn breath followed by an exhalation sighed out from the tower; there were more rustlings and then the voice continued in a flat, unemotional tone.

My name is Adèle Clauvy. I am forty-three years of age, a widow, and until recently I resided at 24 rue des Saints-Pères in the seventh arrondissement. Because of my husband's suicide and the subsequent disclosure that he had swindled large sums from his employer, I derived no benefit from his estate and was forced, therefore, to seek employment.

On February 27, 1905, I presented myself at the Club de Jeu, an exclusive men's preserve on the rue Lisbonne, for an interview with Claude Lecouvreur, Comte de Beaumanoir. The Count received me in a narrow, high-ceilinged room which was dominated by an immense globe showing the continents according to Ptolemy, and whose walls were lined in gilt-lettered volumes all bound in red morocco. Heavy burgundy drapes shut out the winter light, a fire crackled in the hearth. He did not rise, but inclined his head and bade me be seated in the chair facing him beside the fire, and asked for a moment in which to reacquaint himself with my résumé.

He was of middle years and average stature, yet striking in appearance. His morning coat and trousers were at odds with his ragged hair and bristling black beard, both of which were shot through with dramatic streaks of gray, and his features had a hand-whittled look: white pine taken down by a master carver into a high forehead, an aquiline nose and a wide, resolute mouth. On his right hand he wore a massive gold ring, bearing a raised coat of arms, which he slipped on and off as he read; it moved so easily I presumed he had experienced a drastic loss of weight.

He closed the folder and fixed me with a heavy-lidded, hawk-ish stare. "You wish to apply for *both* positions, madame?"

"Yes, Count, if they are compatible. I served as my husband's secretary during our marriage and I am grounded in calculus and trigonometry, as well as the principles of engineering."

"Yes, yes!" he said impatiently. "But the meditation . . . ?"

"As you can see by my résumé, my husband worked nine years with a British firm in India. While there I took up the practice of yoga for reasons of health."

"Are you then a mystic, a devotee of Eastern philosophy?"

"I am Catholic, Count. But I do not find the wisdom of the East incompatible with my faith."

"I am tempted to engage you, madame, solely because it will reduce by one the number of persons I must bring into my home. I have, you see, suffered a . . . a breakdown. My equations have become incomprehensible to me, mere hen scratchings, and I am unable to think about my work in other than the most general and mechanical terms. It is my hope that through an ordering of my notes with the proper assistance I may regain an understanding of the principles involved. But I dare not enlist a fellow scientist or anyone who might—"

"If loyalty is your concern, Count," I interrupted, "I can assure you on that point. For twenty-one years I was loyal to a single cause: my marriage. Now it has foundered and I am at loose ends. I have no wish to remarry and lay flowers upon a second grave. Could I but find some absorbing work, I believe I would be as faithful to it as I am to God and the Republic!"

The Count seemed amused by my speech, as formulated and ritual as it was, as if he recognized how desperate I was for this or any position. He leaned back against the window, smiling. "Do not these loyalties—'God and the Republic'—sometimes contend?" Then, brusque, he said, "Never mind, madame. Loyalty is not my concern in your case. You have too little theory to suit me, and as for the other position, being temporary, it hardly fulfills your own requirements."

"Count! Theory can be learned! I have a logical and orderly mind. If your equations are not absolutely alien to the laws of common sense, I will no doubt be able to provide you with clues to their nature. And is this not exactly what you *do* require?"

At this juncture Mme. Clauvy broke off, less than six minutes after she had begun, in a fit of choking. By the time she made her next statement, darkness had fallen over Paris and the crowd had tripled in size. They milled back and forth, gossiping, questioning each other; small groups huddled around transistor radios listening to the revelations of the media.

There *had* been, it seemed, an Adèle Clauvy residing in the rue des Saints-Pères, but at number 36, not number 24; and her husband had *not* been a suicide but had survived the mysterious disappearance of his wife in 1905 by eleven years. In Quercy investigations were being initiated as to the Comte de Beaumanoir; preliminary research, however, had determined that the title had been vacant since—coincidentally—the year 1905.

Spotlights swept over the face of the tower, and the magnesium brilliance of television lights burned like unholy fires in the midst of the crowd. The bishop of Paris announced that he felt the voice to be nothing more than a prank, but his statement did not deter the spokesman of a charismatic sect from climbing onto one of the piers and proclaiming the Rapture through a bullhorn. Salvador Dali, who had been hired as a special correspondent to report on this most surreal of events, declared it "a sublime act of ventriloquism, vital confirmation of the prophecies of Artaud and the lunatic rituals of Tristan Tzara. Something of the sort," he said, twirling his mustache, "was bound to happen eventually."

At nine thirty-three Mme. Clauvy spoke once again.

I may be dying (she said, her voice tremulous). If so, if my remains are found, then I ask that they be given Christian burial and that a mass be said in my name at the church of St. Francis Xavier. I . . .

I will now continue with my story.

Suffice it to say that I was engaged. I had intended to detail further the events of my interview, hoping thereby to illuminate the Count's character, but perhaps it is unimportant, and besides,

I do not know how much time is left me. . . . So. I will pass over the matter and read an excerpt from my journal.

At this point Mme. Clauvy coughed and cleared her throat, an event which prompted Dali to suggest that an enormous bottle of cough medicine be made available to the tower. "God help us," he said, "if she proves contagious."

April 9, 1905. The train left Orléans Station at 7:40 A.M., on time, and shortly thereafter wound through grassy meadows starred with narcissus. I paid little attention, however, to the scenery; my thoughts were still in a whirl at leaving the rue des Saints-Pères. Though we had lived there for only three years, I had come to rest in those apartments like a stone at the bottom of a long hill, and I had imagined myself growing old amid the tinted photographs and floral wallpaper. As I turned at the door for a final look around, I noticed the shadow of the ivy plant upon the rug. It had always seemed to me the sigil of my marriage, my life, an obscure character drawn in light and shade, elegant and perfectly ordered to its obscurity, but now I saw how unruly it had grown and I had the thought that it had been nourished in its growth by Guillaume's suicide, the cancerous act which had dissolved my quiet existence. I grieved for him, but he had—after all—left me, and so I had reasoned him away to some extent, now equating his loss with the loss of tranquillity, of stability and comfort.

When I roused from this reverie it was late afternoon, and I found the countryside had changed from pleasant meadows into a tortuous waste of limestone cliffs and gorges through which a foaming river plunged: the Dordogne. Now and again the train rose onto a plateau figured by twisting trees and rubbly fields; brown unforested hills lifted from the horizon. "The Causses Quercy," said the conductor, gesturing at the landscape. "The home of wolves, idiots and madmen." I watched with attentiveness as the panoramas unfolded, for though I had known such a region existed, I had not imagined the desolation of the place. Flat stones like ancient dolmens balanced on the edge of precipices and the sheer walls beneath them had been flaked away into great arches. We passed below promontories which the afternoon shadow tricked into the likeness of grimacing faces. Although the sun warmed the window glass, the calcerous reds and whites of the stone seemed to have leached the light of all vitality, and I fancied that should I open the window I might not be able to breathe: the air being so dilute.

Just before sunset we reached the village of La Rocque, a huddle of stone houses at the base of a white cliff sprinkled with the green of juniper bushes growing from its interstices. An old man —Jehan was his name, his pasty face rumpled as a dishrag— conveyed me in a donkey cart to the castle atop the cliff, following a steep trail lined with boulders through which I glimpsed the fissured plain beneath, baked red in the rays of the dying sun. It seemed I was rising to a summit in hell, an idea assisted by the departure of the train as it slithered off into one of the fissures: a howling black worm tunneling into Satan's lined and calloused palm.

The driver left me standing in the courtyard beside my luggage, and though he had been surly and uncommunicative, I was sad to see him go. It was a ruinous, ghostly place, a jumble of stone so haphazardly piled it might have been simply another production of the limestone, the semblance of a castle. The single tower had collapsed into a jagged tooth; the flags were broken and clumps of grass—black in the reddening light—thrust up between them; the walls had dissolved into heaps of rubble. Seeing no one about, I hesitantly mounted a stair which led to a door upon whose lintel crude letters had been incised: THINGS WILL IMPROVE, they read.

The hall within was gloomy, vaulted; my footsteps echoed like pebbles falling in a well. Three great windows to the west glowed scarlet, floating upon the darkness, and there was no furnishing or decoration other than a group of portraits arranged together in a cheap deal border above the hearth. The lowest-hung of these were of the Count, and—separated by a space whose discoloration hinted at a recent removal—two young brunette women in lacy white frocks. They were daintily posed but their faces

were coarse-featured, plump, a trifle lantern-jawed, and they bore
no resemblance to the Count.

"Madame Clauvy!"

Voices chimed in chorus behind me. I turned and saw these
same two girls standing a few paces away, their white frocks
gleaming pale in the accumulating dark; they seemed inset into
the gloom, made distinct from it by some intangible, shimmering
margin, like apparitions. They curtsied—clumsily, I thought—
and swooped at me, danced around me and brushed my cheeks
with touches soft as moth wings.

"I am Mireille," said the taller, and her sister, peering coyly
over her shoulder, said, "And I am Charlotte."

"Oh, we are so pleased, madame—" said Mireille.

"—once more to have a woman to confide in," finished her
sister.

They tittered, clinging together in an embrace. Their eyes
rolled up and they gave breathy gasps that seemed to me feigned
expressions of unbearable delight.

"Come, madame," they said in unison. "We will show you to
your room."

As they ran ahead of me, lifting the hems of their skirts and
giggling, I noticed that their movements were ponderous, and
this—in conjunction with their frilly manners—conveyed a
comic impression: two heavy-ankled, pigeon-breasted shopgirls
with blotchy complexions masquerading as princesses.

I followed them down a lamplit corridor, turning right three
times. Many of the doors stood open; within the rooms I saw
broken chairs, shattered vases, empty packing crates, all cobwebbed and embedded in sticky-looking shadows. Seeing this dilapidation, listening to the tittering of the two girls—in the echoing corridor it sounded eerie and distant as the chirping of bats—
I thought longingly of the little inn I had seen below in the
village.

We turned right a fourth time (the corridor, apparently, was
laid out in a maze pattern, or else, by my reckoning, we should
have found ourselves back in the great hall) and came to a room
from whose door spilled a fan of brilliant light. Charlotte and

Mireille grasped my arms. "Oh, madame," they chorused. "We hope you will be pleased!" And they pressed me forward into the most richly furnished room I have ever seen.

A Gobelin tapestry hung upon one wall—hunters and unicorns rendered in gold thread on green backing—and the bed was big as a barge, canopied in embroidered silk; the escritoire was of ormolu-mounted kingwood, the mounts incorporating a design of cornflowers, and a fire screen of brass and faiencework fronted the hearth; walnut chairs upholstered in blue-and-silver damask, a rosewood cabinet faced with marquetry panels depicting cranes and lilies, a lacquered ebony night table . . . all reflected by an enormous pier glass mirror surmounted by gilt angels. If I were forced to categorize the furnishings, I might say their style was neorococo, but nothing in the room fitted together; it was as if I had stepped inside a jewelry box and stood among looped strands of pearls and tumbled, gaudy rings.

Charlotte and Mireille fluttered about me, displaying this or that ornament, and I began to feel more at ease in their company. On first encounter I had suspected them of mocking me by their show of delight, but now their giddy manners and bow-shaped mouths and rouged cheeks took on a clownish aspect. These sweet, dizzy creatures, I thought, have souls of crystallized sugar which sway in them and make them ring innocent and giggling. . . . Or perhaps they shared a single such soul, for though one was taller, the other heavier, they were both large and lumbering, and I could detect no difference in personality between them.

"Why do you wish to learn meditation?" I asked as we sat upon the bed.

"Oh, we must, we must!" they sang out. "It is essential to our Purpose!" They embraced, kissed—a peck upon the lips—and pressed their cheeks together, giggling, as if they were sharing a delicious secret.

When I asked them to explain this "Purpose," they made sad eyes and drooping mouths and left me, saying that they must join their father in the laboratory and that he would welcome me himself in the morning.

Alone now, I am discomforted by the room; it glitters from

every angle, too full of sheen and glimmer for the eye to settle, and I have a sense of being encysted within the castle, like a gemstone lodged in the rib cage of a gray, moldering skeleton. Furthermore, the view from the window is quite disconcerting. Directly below lies the shadowy mouth of a pit some fifty feet or so in width, and beyond it, scattered over the fissured plateau on which the castle rests, rises a veritable forest of metal rods tipped with crystals. It is midnight and I can no longer see them in the darkness, but at sunset the crystals were surrounded by a faint auroral display, refractions of ruby light. At the edge of the plateau, also invisible to me now, stands a wind-eroded monolith, runneled like an old tooth.

This awful landscape must have buried within it a magnet which attracts the iron of my soul, for on first glimpsing it I could hardly turn my eyes away, and since then it has flitted constantly before my mind's eye; it seems familiar, yet I have never seen its like before, and this sense of familiarity has nothing in common with the sensation of *déjà vu*. . . . No, it is as if this place were the site of some great event—I can only conceive of it as a tragedy, a desecration—now slipped from my memory. The long journey by train, the strains of recent months, the ruined castle and its odd inhabitants: perhaps these elements conspire against my sensibility. Still, I cannot fully reject the idea that outside my bedroom window lies the relic of an otherworldly Golgotha.

"I must refresh myself," said Mme. Clauvy. "Perhaps I will sleep. I—" She sighed, exasperated. "I was about to ask your assistance in diagnosing my injuries. You people, imagined as you are, are growing quite real to me."

The crowd swelled to nearly sixty thousand during the night, becoming as various as a small city, having slums where raucous men and women drank and scuffled, suburbs populated by families with picnic hampers and radios, and exclusive neighborhoods centered about the television trucks. A patch of ground was cleared in front of the tower and a podium erected for the benefit of those politicians and officials who wished to address the crowd. They joked and made light of the voice, but scientists returning from the upper levels frowned and declined interviews, and one—when asked if they had learned who had perpetrated the hoax—replied, "It is no hoax," before being escorted away.

Whenever a bulletin was released, the crowd grew restive, for the news, though sparse, was unsettling. In Quercy soldiers had cordoned off the road leading to the Beaumanoir estate, and the village of La Rocque had been evacuated. Scientists and military personnel had descended into the caverns beneath the castle, but little was known of their investigations; there were, however, rumors of casualties; the local stringer for *Le Figaro* claimed to have seen one of the victims, and described the man as being "mauled, ripped, as if by a wild animal." The report was labeled "irresponsible" by a government spokesman.

Foreign reaction was negligible and generally lighthearted in tone. President Reagan's off-the-record yet highly publicized remark concerning Frenchwomen and big erections was echoed in equally trivial, though more tactful, statements by the European heads of state; but, belying their deferential attitudes, grim-faced ambassadors paid late-night calls upon François Mitterrand and —according to informed sources—were sent away without having gained an audience.

As morning approached and the tower emerged from the dark, appearing skeletal, like a charcoal sketch against the backdrop of gray clouds, the crowd quieted and the atmosphere upon the Champ de Mars was that of a shrine thronged by pilgrims awaiting a predicted visitation. Lovers and children slept curled in each other's arms, and even the most fanatical of the religious organizations who had paraded all night long carrying a banner depicting burning hands and bearing the slogan "Hell Is Real"— even they sat calmly, listening to the brimstone hiss of the tower, smiling, for they guessed it to be the sputtering of a mighty fuse which would bring them hard upon salvation.

At 6:41 A.M. Mme. Clauvy again rustled her papers and addressed the world.

I have passed some difficult hours (she said, firm and dispassionate). I do not know what this portends, but I had best speed things along and continue my story without preamble.

Despite their flightiness, Charlotte and Mireille approached their lessons with zeal and, in a few short weeks, had gained an astounding mastery of meditative technique; indeed, had I allowed it, they would have spent all their hours immersed in a deep trance, sitting cross-legged on the floor of my bedroom like outsized dolls posed for an imaginary tea party. Their devotion to the mysterious "Purpose" was unflagging.

My work with the Count, however, did not prove so instantly successful. His notes were a hodgepodge of poorly detailed experiments and scrawled equations, many of these inscribed in a private system of notation to which he did not recall the key, and though I studied volume after volume of mathematical theory in my efforts to unscramble them, I made no progress whatever. As he had stated during our first interview, his own knowledge had been reduced to the merely general, and he offered me an incoherent, almost mystical description of his process.

"It seems," he said, "that I have performed a magical operation rather than carrying out a scientific investigation, that for a period of years I did exactly the right thing at the right time, and by virtue of this incredible run of luck I have effected a law, discovered a force to which proofs are not essential."

At first I believed him mad, in futile pursuit of a knowledge which had never existed, but I did not voice my opinion because I cherished my position too greatly to risk his displeasure. On gaining admittance to his laboratory, however, my doubts were in part eroded. The extensiveness and good condition of his equipment reflected both an organized approach and consequential abilities.

The laboratory was situated beneath the castle but could be entered only by riding down on a winch-controlled wooden platform into a vast limestone cavern (this being the pit I had seen from my bedroom window), a section of whose roof had collapsed and whose rubble-strewn floor lay over two hundred feet below. I have no head for heights and, eventually, dreading these daily descents, I transferred a few belongings to the laboratory and often spent an entire week without leaving the caverns. But I must admit that the descents were spectacular. At the mouth and from every rib of this gloomy funnel draped shadowy streamers of fern, clematis and scolopendrium. The walls were hewn precipitously or in corbeled projections joined by the stratifications, one bed overlying the next, and on looking up from the bottom I could see the light strangely sifted, almost violet, illuminating the walls with reflections. By night the sky appeared as a ceiling set with golden nails. In the coating of crystallized calcerous material were numbers of holes the size of hazel nuts where lived small red spiders whose heads were bigger than their bodies; they spun webs in the shape of sunbursts to snare the snow-white flies dreamily flitting about on lacy and disproportionately large wings. I attempted to catch some of these flies, hoping to preserve them in a paper cornet, but they were so delicate that they seemed to melt away between my fingers.

A short passage led from the ruined cavern into a second and smaller chamber—an antechamber really, for its far wall was sealed by an iron door beyond which lay the transmitter. The ceiling was low, the stone gray and overlaid by a verdigris of moss, and along the walls stood banks of gauges and dials encased in cabinets of black iron; they indicated—so the Count informed me—levels of energy stored by the "solar collectors" (these, then, were the metal rods tipped with crystals I had seen from my window). He made the peculiar statement that solar energy had once been a common source of power, but when I asked him for clarification he dismissed the topic with a curt gesture.

By day I sat at a wooden table beside the iron door, poring over the Count's notes, which were kept loose in crates. He often joined me there, occasionally remarking upon some dimly recalled principle of etheric science; then, frowning at my feeble attempts at calculation, he would pace about the cavern, lecturing, while I trailed behind, my notebook in hand, ready to jot down any sudden insight his words might convey. I felt as if I were reading tea leaves rather than employing my logic; the problem was too ill defined for logic, and his words were tantalizing shapes coming clear in a cloudy liquid, fading before I could wholly make them out.

"The ether is all-pervasive, madame," he said at the advent of his first such lecture. "It spreads throughout time as well as space; it is the primary constituent of the universe: the least atom, the world, the stars, are but the perceptible analogue of its interaction with time, of time's excitation of the etheric structures—those patterns underlying every event and phenomenon. It is the medium by which all energies are transmitted—heat, light, sound . . . Even thought, madame!"

He stared at me, suddenly aghast and uncomprehending.

How odd it seems in memory: his morning coat (he was always formally attired), the sheer planes of the rock walls and the ferns drooping from the cracks, the needles of the gauges flickering behind him as if measuring his decibel level—all these shared an exotic context, a strange coherence into which my role as the recorder of genius fitted naturally. . . . And yet we had no relationship. Oh, I was his tool and he my support, not an uncommon sort of union between man and woman, but we were shadowy creatures to each other, as might be the oppositional deities of some primitive faith. His stares were *often* aghast and uncomprehending. God knows what he saw in my place.

"We live in an ocean of ether," he went on, "and yet have no more consciousness or conception of it than a fish dwelling in the most profound deep might have of water. It was my original intention to construct a wireless radio—and I did so, though its use as such is impractical—but I soon determined that could I perceive the nature of the etheric structures, study them, then I might lay bare the secrets of time itself and so effect miraculous changes.

"My first notions as to the nature of the ether were, to say the least, whimsical, though perhaps they were correct. For example: it occurred to me that deserts and wastelands might be instances of weak interactions between time and the ether, and that in such places it might be an easier task to scry out the structures; the very lack of life and event seemed a signal of this weak interac-

tion, and not simply the result of poor soil and atmospheric con-
ditions which are, in themselves, the result of etheric distur-
bances. The fact that deserts are the seat of legends, ghosts and
mirages also seemed of moment: these, too, might be signals of
the weak interaction. And, since my home stood in the center of
the Causses Quercy, I felt ordained and destined for the
work. . . ."

He would ramble on in this or a similar vein for hours, waxing
rapturous in his evocations of the ether, but succeeding only in
confusing me. Once, when I asked him to interpret a symbol
from his notes, he glared at it as if it were a spider and said, "It is
not clear to me, madame. At any rate, it is not important. Calculation is the least element of any understanding."

At last, four months after my arrival, he took me fully into his
confidence.

It was early morning, shortly before eight o'clock. The Count
had provided me with a small stove for cooking and making tea,
and I was just clearing breakfast from the wooden table when he
came into the cavern. I had begun to enjoy my life belowground;
it was as if I were inhabiting the base camp of some far-ranging
expedition, a Himalayan cave, perhaps, in trackless Tibet; and
my daily routines—washing dishes in the trickle which sprang
from the rock wall beyond the entrance, sweeping the pebbly
floor, performing my rough ablutions—gave me a sense of both
normalcy and adventure which I found stimulating. I believe the
Count was aware of my pleasure in these routines, and so, on that
particular morning, he waited patiently until I had completed my
tasks.

"You find the . . . rather formal behavior of my daughters a
bit peculiar, do you not, madame?"

I said that I thought them a trifle ingrown; that they might
benefit from less solitude, more friends of their own age.

He laughed. "Eight months ago you would have thought them
typical, exemplary of their class. You would have recognized
their manner as a language in which each flutter, each cooing
breath and lowered lash expressed a delicate shade of meaning. A
purely feminine language, infinitely revealing of self and circum-

stance, a construct of such subtle—Ah!" He shook his head as if clearing it of a delightful vapor. "Once all women of breeding employed it, but the world has changed, Madame Clauvy. I have changed it." He looked up to the roof, abstracted. "I have changed the character of the ether and, therefore, altered time. Do you believe me?"

"It hardly seems reasonable," I replied, choosing my words with care, not wishing to antagonize him. "Things are as always, at least to my recollection."

"Reasonable! Perhaps not; nonetheless, it is true. The dilapidation of this castle in comparison to its original state, madame, may be likened to the current condition of the world relative to *its* original. There was peace, nations planned together, famines and plagues were swiftly resolved by their concerted efforts, and there was time for rarefied pursuits and subtle developments of the loutish customs which now exist between men. My daughters' behavior is a survival of that world, as are a thousand other things: a scrap of parchment bearing an indecipherable alphabet; a crystal artifact in the shape of a skull; an unclassified fossil; a fragment of legend now misinterpreted as fantasy. But my knowledge of etheric transmission did not survive." He rose and began to pace about, illuminating his discourse with flowery gestures more appropriate to a poet than a scientist. "Thought is an expression of the ether, nothing less, one which our brains amplify, personify, and when I changed the ether, I changed the character of thought. So. Though my mind crawls with the old knowledge, it is as if the convolutions of my brain have writhed up into new patterns like spidery, misspelled words and will no longer act as conduits, as if the entire world were packed into my skull except for the element of my understanding. Perhaps I have altered the nature of physical laws, perhaps the principles of my world's science now comprise the arcana of this new world's magic. Or perhaps only my understanding has changed. It scarcely matters.

"How beautiful it was; still I sought to improve it!" For a moment I thought he might burst into tears. His voice quavered, but he steeled himself and continued. "Immortality, Madame Clauvy! That was my goal. I intended to produce a longevity drug by stimulating certain researches in the year 1763. From my studies of etheric structures I had derived a mathematics by means of which I could calculate the exact action necessary to produce any effect. But I failed to consider one aspect of the operation. My wife, who had volunteered to carry out my instructions in the past—Do not look so horrified, madame! This was her work as well as mine, as now it is my daughters'. My wife . . . my wife went mad during the transmission and, on her arrival in 1763, took other actions than those I had proposed. I cannot be certain of all the changes that have resulted; I have changed as much as the world. But I have a strange, doubled knowledge of a number of events. I recall, for instance, studying the French Revolution when I was a child, yet I am convinced beyond the shadow of a doubt that such a terror was never visited upon the France of my birth. . . ."

"Count!" I choked back the remainder of my words.

"You think me deluded, madame?" He stood, angry. "Tomorrow you shall have all the proof you require, but this may suffice for now." He drew a slim leather-bound volume from his coat and tossed it on the table. "Page eighty-three," he said, and stalked from the cavern.

I did not feel at ease in the laboratory; that afternoon I returned to my bedroom and there inspected the book. It was entitled *Memoirs of a Court Physician*, by Dr. Jules Michelet, and was profusely illustrated with engravings. The engraving on page eighty-three depicted a plump-cheeked, lantern-jawed woman in her forties; I immediately noticed the resemblance to the Count's daughters. The text recorded the case history of this woman who, clad in a lacy white dress, had appeared before the palace of Versailles one day in 1763, screaming and pulling her hair. Dr. Michelet had treated her for twelve years until her death by heart failure. During that time her behavior was hysteric, but there were periods of clarity in which she managed coherent conversation. She described an awful solitude, a term of total disembodiment, blind, deaf, bereft of all her senses, and she made constant reference to her husband, Claude. Louis XV, whose personal physician Dr. Michelet was, delighted in the woman, calling her his "white mystery," and, whenever her mind cleared sufficiently, he brought her into the throne room, where she instructed the ladies of the court in matters of style and grace, and made pronouncements as to the future of France: pronouncements which, it was said, had a profound effect upon the young dauphin.

When I had done reading, I sat at my window until the sun dropped low on the horizon. I could not accept the Count's tale, yet I could not deny it. Somehow it rang true in spite of the paucity of evidence: two odd girls, a laboratory, an entry in an old book. And it was obvious that Charlotte and Mireille believed it; I understood at last their zealous attention to my lessons —they thought that the meditative techniques would protect their minds during transmission, allow them to pass serenely back through time while contemplating nothing. If, indeed, the tale were true, I doubted whether a mantra would prove an efficient safeguard. I was alternately disbelieving and horrified, too confused to grasp the possibilities involved, but as I watched the sun redden the limestone plateau, shadows deepening the fissures which, sinuous as serpents, radiated out from the castle walls, the ruby glints above the "solar collectors," the grotesque, blood-colored monolith standing forth like the victorious king upon a demon's chessboard, that terrible, alien landscape seemed the ultimate credential of both the Count's theories *and* his madness.

A soft thump issued from the tower. "I am very weary," said Mme. Clauvy. "Be it day or night where you stand, I wish you well of it."

The overcast lightened; a pale, blurred sun showed through a veil of gray cloud. Exhausted by the long night, nerves set on edge by the news blackout initiated in Quercy shortly before dawn, the crowd became agitated. Children cried, drunken fistfights erupted and the religious zealots began marching once again, hoisting high their banner and knocking people from their path. Amid this unrest Marion Choiseul, the nominal leader of the French right, spoke from the tower podium at 9 A.M.

"What is happening in Quercy?" he asked mildly. "If this is a hoax, then why the secrecy?"

He paused, letting crowd noise build to a babble of shouted opinion, then gripped the lectern and himself shouted: "Because this is no hoax! Adèle Clauvy is *not* the invention of an extremist group! She is a brave Frenchwoman who with her last strength is informing us of a great tragedy. But one which she has willed us the power to repair!"

Camera shutters snicked; the crowd held silent.

Choiseul brushed back a lock of hair from his eyes. "But I wonder if the Mitterrand government wishes us to repair it."

A handful of voices answered, "No!"

"No!" said Choiseul. "They do not! They—"

An automatic rifle chattered; Choiseul was blown backward off the podium as though pulled by an invisible cord. Screams rose from the crowd, and, as more shots sounded, sixty thousand people fled the Champ de Mars, scattering in every direction like iron filings repelled by a magnet whose polarity has been suddenly reversed. Within minutes the field was empty of all but the police, the dead and the wounded—two hundred and twenty-seven men, women and children shot, trampled, drowned in the duck ponds at the base of the tower—and those who clung to them, mourning. Sirens brayed, ambulances and medical personnel poured forth from the Hôpital des Invalides, and soon black mortuary vans rumbled up and began removing the litter of bodies which lay sprawled in pitiful attitudes upon the grass.

Twenty-five minutes after the outbreak of violence—under the orders of General Trinquier and commanded by Colonel Marc Chalandon—a detachment of paratroops arrived by helicopters and erected sandbagged fortifications at access points to the Champ de Mars. Patrols evacuated all buildings within a half-mile of the tower, even the hospital, thereby ensuring that Mme. Clauvy would be heard by none but the chosen; sentry posts were established along the various avenues. By 2 P.M. the last house had been cleared and the soldiers sat at ease, smoking, listening to transistor radios as had the crowd before them. The Security Council of the United Nations had met in emergency session—

the French delegate not in attendance—and had passed a resolution asking that France open the caverns in Quercy to an international inspection team; the Secretary-General had called for a ban on etheric research. From Quercy came unsubstantiated reports of a battle atop the plateau where stood the castle of the Comte de Beaumanoir.

The great hissing from the tower dominated the lesser sounds of radios and men talking, and a strong wind blew up, now and then outvoicing the hiss, modulating it with an ominous vowel so that it seemed the tower was pronouncing a sad, sibilant word over and over again. Paper cups and bits of cellophane drifted across the grass. The soldiers turned up their collars against the rain which began spitting, speckling the cement walkways with dark drops, distant bells tolled half past two, and Mme. Clauvy coughed.

Good morning (she said, sounding more cheerful than usual), or good evening, as the case may be. I have not yet adjusted to speaking to an invisible audience and—of course—this is the reason I write the text of my statements; otherwise I would "er" and "ah" and appear quite foolish. Be that as it may, it may amuse you to know how variously I imagine you. This morning, for instance, I picture a stand draped with bunting and fat politicians in silk hats seated upon it, and crowds of young schoolgirls clad in pink and yellow and blue frocks surrounding them like fields of wild flowers. Yesterday, however, I imagined grim, silent ranks of listeners such as might be seen at a grave site. I hope the former is the reality.

I will continue by reading another excerpt from my journal. It is markedly different in tone from my preceding statement, but you must remember I had just witnessed a scientific miracle and I stood in awe of its creator.

August 22, 1905. I have seen the transmitter. Surely it is the marvel of our age, and more surely yet the name of Claude Lecouvreur will rank even above those of Aristotle and Galileo.

This morning he guided me beyond the iron door into a chamber whose gravelly floor sloped down to a black lake; beached upon its margin was a folding canoe—an Osgood, I believe—of much the same sort which Guillaume brought with us to India for the purpose of boating upon the Ganges. As we drifted out upon the lake the Count lit a magnesium lantern mounted on the prow and a thin smoke spiraled up from it, dissipating before it reached the vast cupola glittering with stalactites. At the far end of the lake the water flowed away into utter blackness between two towering stalagmitic columns, and we entered into a narrows. Though it did not seem wide enough to admit us, the canoe was somewhat compressible and we thrust at the walls with both hands, pushing the craft along. The membranes groaned, the canvas grated, but we succeeded in squeezing through and issued into an underground river. Here the walls arched overhead and were banked and shelved at a height of ten feet above the water; from the edges of the shelves rose clusters of tiny stalagmites, like thorns.

"Look there, madame!" The Count's face was ghoulish, underlit by the lantern; he pointed down into the water. Pale lightnings flickered beneath the surface, branching, forking, then vanishing, as if electric charges were being sent through the river.

"In effect," said the Count, "we are already within the field of the transmitter. Its boundaries are diffuse. Even here some of the matter is constantly being excited into an etheric state."

He instructed me to extinguish the lantern; when I did so a vivid white light sprang into view around a distant bend; it ebbed and flowed along the walls as if its source were pulsing. At that moment we were drifting toward a shelf tipped by a thick, blunt stalagmite—or so I'd supposed it—for as the light struck it, it shifted, stood and assumed the shape of a winged man. I am certain of the wings, I could see their sharp ribs in silhouette jutting above his shoulders. I could not make out his features but felt the pressure of his gaze, as if a hole had been punched through a window onto a wintry night. His shaggy head turned, following us, and as we passed beneath the shelf he stretched out a taloned hand. . . . I drew back from him, falling into the bottom of the canoe, nearly overturning it—or did I fall, was I not flung back by the dark force of his gesture? I guessed his reach was infinite, extending from some chill corruption at the heart of things, yet when I recovered and looked again there was only a haze of black, swirling points which misted away.

I turned to the Count in alarm, but he waved airily. "It was nothing, madame, or scarcely more. These phantoms rise out from the ether like genies from a magic lamp. The weight of our perceptions, it seems, will not allow them to exist."

He did not reassure me. At every echoing drip, every plop of a falling pebble, I cast about for the sight of another winged devil, but saw only the tiny, thornlike stalagmites doubled in shadow on the walls.

"Originally," said the Count, "I wondered if the ether might not have to be watched over, maintained like a sacred fire in order to prevent these apparitions from fully materializing. But I have since been absent for extended periods and there has been no such manifestation."

He rambled on about the odd things he had seen pop up and disappear along the river: beasts of every description, strange men and women; the winged man, he said, appeared more frequently than most. I asked him to desist after a while, finding this catalog of illusions unnerving.

I would have sworn the heart of the light lay around the next bend, straight ahead, but we must have turned half a dozen bends on an inward-twisting course until, finally, we beached beneath a stalagmitic ridge above which the white radiance brimmed. The walls of the surrounding cavern were fabulous evolutions of pinkish limestone: thousands of cunning formations appearing at one moment to be lilies or gargoyles, at the next transforming into a lion's face or a castle turret; in the pulsing light they seemed to flow constantly in upon themselves, like the coils of serpents, then flow back out into a new image. Depended from the ceiling by an iron bolt was an oval cage, also iron, whose floor was the upper terminus of a slender crystal column, unfaceted, rising forty feet out of the light.

Excited as I had never seen him, the Count dragged me halfway up the ridge to a metal cabinet set with dials and switches. Cables snaked from its sides over the ridgetop.

"It is unreasonable that these controls still function," he said. "The cables vanish into the light, I no longer know to what they lead. Yet when I adjust the controls, the effects are as I would predict. Now here, madame"—he indicated a fine mesh grille— "the wireless. One presses this switch, adjusts these dials for latitude and longitude—this, the red dial, governs the direction in time—and one may then whisper into the ears of dead kings or shout the truth to unborn multitudes. At present it is focused upon the Eiffel Tower. Among all the hideous constructs of this world, none is more opposite to my own in terms of style and grace. Should I be unable to correct my error, I will then attempt to persuade the world with an oracle: a great voice speaking to the masses, urging change. And when I have done, I will—by simply ending the transmission—destroy the tower, thereby satisfying my sense of esthetics as well as giving a signal of my power."

I had barely listened, absorbed by the flickering patterns of light around the crystal column, much like those I had seen coursing through the underground river, but now I asked how he would manage such a feat.

"As I have told you, the use of the transmitter as a wireless is totally impractical. The wave shaped through the ether gradually excites the matter of the receiver into an etheric state. When the transmission is ended, the wave completes its action and the receiver disperses. . . . It vanishes! But this is a parlor trick, madame. Come and look upon the face of—" He laughed. "I do not know what to call it: the All-Pervasive, life, the yang, the active principle unfolding. . . ."

Atop the ridge the light enveloped me in a sparkling white fog, and I thought I saw the ghost of a machine buried in it far below: a vague assemblage of bristling rods and domes. But it did not hold my attention. My eye was captured by the flickers of light within the ether—I say "light," yet I do not believe that was their nature. They were expressions of an intense opacity like those tangles of cells which drift across the field of vision when one stands too quickly, and though in their forkings and branchings they reminded me of electric charges, they had not the jaggedness of electricity, reminding one more of the sinuous fissures spreading over the limestone plateau. They were brief flashes, but I found if I concentrated and tracked a single branching, then I could follow it out and out. . . .

Suddenly, I had the sensation—absolute, complete to the least detail—of standing in a cottage garden. The year was 1893. . . . I knew the year, knew everything about the circumstance: that the village was Les Roziers in Languedoc, that the garden and cottage belonged to Giselle Gambièze, a grandmotherly widow. Hawthorn leaves lifted overhead, their undersides arabesqued by worm trails; rosebushes lined a whitewashed wall. The creak and rattle of an oxcart—I could smell the oxen's damp skin— sounded from the lane. Then all this was swept away by a second vision: Paris, 1387, a gray sky hung with reeking smokes, a child's pale face peering from a shadowed door, a white hand snatching him back inside a house of undressed stone, grimy straw poking up through the muck of a muddy lane. And then a third vision so brief that I could not fully orient myself, and recall of it only a starry night.

"What did you see?" The Count pulled me down behind the ridge, away from the light.

I told him, stammering, and asked for an explanation.

"Explain? Things exist without explanation, Madame Clauvy. We pin them to our minds with the legend of cause and effect. Only you have seen what you have seen, and you will always see those exact same sights. . . . Those and more. I dared not let you look too long, it becomes disorienting. But they are junctures at which you—you alone—may take action and alter history, alter the nature of things. I see different sights entirely."

He sat down on a projection of limestone and gazed up at the white radiance, so bright that the ridge seemed to be crumbling away beneath it, becoming transparent.

"Exposure to this distilled etheric state affects our brains individually, or, one might say, the patterned pathways of our brains are intimate reflections of certain etheric structures which—when we perceive them here—resonate within us and unveil their secrets. There is a kind of connectivity between these 'visions' as you call them, and after long years of study I managed to derive a highly personal mathematics, a methodology of correct actions. . . ."

I lost track of his explanation, still enraptured by my glimpse into the ether, for what I had seen was not so flat and uninvolving as I have described. The completeness of the knowledge: that was the wonderful, enrapturing thing. I know not a fraction as much about the specific circumstances of my own life as I did about each successive vision. I could have—had this been my focus—enumerated the atoms in every hawthorn leaf and called to mind the date of that Parisian child's first communion, and the knowledge was a rich potency in my thoughts, as if . . .

Mme. Clauvy's voice faltered. "As if my brain had been steeped in a magic fluid which . . . which allowed me infinite perception. I . . . I saw the shapes of others' lives . . . others' lives all spreading clear as cracks in a stone from . . . this . . . one moment. . . ." Then a faint moan.

The hiss from the tower continued unabated, and throughout the afternoon Mme. Clauvy could be heard moaning in delirium. Night fell, the tower lights remained dark, and spotlights on the Champ de Mars and at the various sentry posts played over the avenues and empty buildings.

Colonel Chalandon sat in his tent with an aide listening to the radio. The assassination of François Mitterrand and his cabinet had just been announced, and Generals Trinquier, Cadoudal and Massu had all claimed ascendancy to the position of head of state. Tank units were battling each other on the outskirts of Paris. There was no news from Quercy.

"Even the generals are mad," said Chalandon. "One might have trusted old Trinquier, but Massu . . . ? He rides about in his jeep as if it were a chariot. And Cadoudal! Hah! I've heard he wears his wife's underclothing to staff meetings!"

The aide looked startled but made no reply.

Automatic rifles stuttered along the boulevard des Invalides and Chalandon grimaced. "I swore after Algiers I'd never kill another Frenchman. But what can I do? The damned code words change every fifteen minutes and I don't know who's changing them. Orders to leave, orders to stay . . . Ahh!"

The radio crackled with the latest bulletin: the Russian ambassador to the United Nations had declared that his government now felt the existence of the transmitter posed a threat to its national security. He harangued the "military elitists who are savaging their own country" and hinted at strategic reprisals unless the caverns were opened at once.

"My God!" said Chalandon. "And here we sit listening to a dead woman moan!"

"We'd better check the perimeter, Colonel," said the aide, holding up his wrist so that Chalandon could see his watch.

"Why not?" Chalandon stood, bumping his head on the canvas, swiping at it angrily. He checked his sidearm. "Let's go! What the devil, eh?"

The spotlights flared over the bullet-shattered windows of the Hôpital des Invalides, flashed over the Quai d'Orsay, illuminating black wavelets on the Seine, and struck like shining swords along the avenues; and when Mme. Clauvy next spoke at eight minutes before midnight, it was as if her voice rang out from a central darkness encircled by outward-looking, fiery eyes.

My pain is gone (she said). I feel translucent, tenuous, as if my body were filled with the white light from the transmitter. I am dying. I suppose I should take advantage of these moments of clarity and conclude my tale, yet it no longer seems urgent. I can barely remember why I began . . . my humanitarian motives, my desire for justice . . . Something. Perhaps simply because I did not wish to die alone: a circumstance to which I am now quite resigned. There is no reason to finish, my secrets are out. But attend me. I will at least satisfy whatever curiosity I have roused in you as to my own conclusion.

I moved my possessions into the cavern containing the transmitter and each day I studied the visions deriving from the etheric structures, each day learning more, both of their nature and of the machine's particulars. An iron staircase—I had not noticed it on my first visit, being preoccupied with the light—could be lowered like a drawbridge from the wall and thus access gained to the cage atop the crystal column: the "amplifier," as the Count called it. Small crystals were set into the bars of the cage, and these, the Count explained, must be replaced after each transmission; he also informed me that twelve hours must be allowed to elapse between transmissions in order to replenish the levels of solar energy, but he was not certain whether either of these factors comprised a scientific necessity or whether they were merely the call and response of some technological ritual.

Scraps of iron lay scattered atop the ridge, left over from the construction, and on one occasion the Count placed an iron sheet within the cage and made it vanish by depressing an orange lever on the control cabinet; it rippled and dissipated into an odd, smoky shape before completely disappearing.

"I dare not send it into time," he said. "Who knows what repercussions even a piece of iron might have? The orange lever effects only the excitation of the matter and its dispersal into the ether. An experimental stage of the device."

I began to see that certain of the Count's equations—in the way they branched across the pages—bore a striking resemblance to the etheric structures, and I wondered whether they might not be maps as much as calculations. When considered in this light they seemed to express themselves more clearly, and I was led to assign values to the most frequently appearing of the characters. Not only was my knowledge growing, but it occurred to me that I was becoming more intelligent, that this particular knowledge fertilized my mind, and so I had confidence in my intuitions; they had the quality of illuminations, messages from an area of my brain newly awakened. At length I presented my charts and graphs to the Count and—as I had expected, by process of a further intuition—this amalgam of half-constructed data acted to restore his understanding.

At first he puzzled over my figures, but then, striking his forehead as if in punishment for some foolishness, he seized them up and sequestered himself with the transmitter for three days, returning once for blankets and provisions. On the morning of the

fourth day he wandered into the cavern, unshaven, looking
stunned. He saw me and beamed, ran to my side and would—I
think—have embraced me, but stopped short as if he had recalled
some regulation against it.

"Madame, you have done it! We have done it! My original
conceit—immortality, the restoration of my world—these are as
nothing to the operation I have devised!"

He painted a picture of man perfected, godlike, immortal, pur-
suing a course of harmony and infinite invention throughout the
universe, and told me that one of my errant calculations had
provided the keystone for his utopic design. He was in a fever to
begin and asked whether his daughters were prepared (this was
to be, apparently, a two-part operation) and I said that I would
like to reassure myself in this regard. . . . You may wonder how
I could so casually join with him in sending two young women
on such a perilous enterprise, but my glimpses into the ether had
bolstered my opinion of meditation as a protective measure: I
had found that the repetition of my own mantra before studying
the etheric structures enabled me better to assimilate the welter
of detail they supplied. And besides, you must remember how in
awe I stood of him and his creation; despite his supercilious manner, I actually entertained the thought of a romance.

I am not certain when my admiration for him began to wane,
when I began to doubt both the feasibility and the intent of his
project, but I believe it must have been during one of our meals
together. These were served by Charlotte and Mireille in the
kitchen: a gloomy, slit-windowed room haunted by two dark ma-
hogany china closets, creaking pantry doors, and a huge black
iron stove which brooded like Cerberus in a pall of woodsmoke
and made me think of the vague machine at the heart of the
transmitter, seeming—by virtue of solidity, anyway—its antithe-
sis. The Count and I sat at opposite ends of the table, studying
each other through the branches of a silver candelabrum whose
holders were serpent mouths, and Charlotte and Mireille flitted
between us like ghostly white moths, cooing and sighing at my
reactions to their cooking.

When they served their father, however, they whispered as

they laid the dishes before him, and these whispers had the rhythmic regularity of a canticle. Once, when their whispers grew particularly fervent, I caught the words ". . . the brand, our father . . ." and a few seconds later I heard ". . . the lion in the forest. . . ." They hovered beside him while he ate, their faces ecstatic, eyes half closed, and from time to time he would lock gazes with them for long moments, and all their faces would clench and twitch as if they were restraining deep emotion. I came to believe these looks were freighted with salacious meaning, resonant of a disturbing relationship between them which I had not previously suspected.

And once, while taking a morning stroll through the weedy little vineyard which bordered the precipice overlooking La Rocque, its leaves blighted with phylloxera and its trellises weathered gray as bones, fractured and leaning, I spied the Count staring out over the limestone plain. He appeared to be in a contemplative mood, his hands clasped behind him, but on hearing my step he whirled around, his face dark and contorted with rage, and raised his fist as if to strike me. I had the idea he had been furious before my arrival, indulging a fury, enjoying his hatred of the sunlight falling too sweetly for his tastes upon the harsh stone. After a moment he mastered himself and begged my forgiveness, saying that he had been thinking about his wife, about the impending loss of his daughters, and had been overcome by grief and frustration. But I could not put from mind his first reaction: yes, he *had* been furious before noticing me, and then he had grown more furious still, joyously so. I might have been an ancient enemy fallen at last into his clutches.

There were dozens of similar incidents, similar in that they conveyed to me a sense of the Count's alienism, and I began to doubt the picture he had painted of both the gracious world he had inhabited and the utopic future he intended. How could I trust the vision of a man so different from myself, one whom I essentially disliked? What sort of world had produced creatures such as Charlotte and Mireille, who—no matter how subtle a language their frothy gestures implied—seemed to me inalterably bovine and stupid? If they were the Count's ideal of grace, why then his dream of utopia might well be flawed, a far cry from my own. And what if he wished to create a demonic circumstance rather than a paradisaical one? I doubted even my own doubts: perhaps they were simply the result of boredom, for since the Count's understanding had been restored, my sole occupation had been the tutelage of his daughters, and, in truth, they needed no further instruction: I had not told the Count.

And then, waking one morning in my resplendent bedroom (I had taken to sleeping there more often than not), in stretching I knocked over the photograph of Guillaume which I kept on the night table. I reached down for it and—the second I touched it—I knew to my soul that he was alive! That I had left him, not the reverse. Alive! This despite the vivid memories I retained of his suicide, of my mourning. At first I thought this knowledge the tag ends of a dream, but it grew in me and soon I could not determine which of the memories I most apprehended as a dream. Shadowy poles crossed in my brain, sparked and rushed apart, crossed again, dueling for the possession of my logic. I fell to my knees, borne down by two contending griefs. At one moment I agonized over my abandonment of Guillaume, and the next I felt again the sick, sodden, cold emptiness weighting down my chest, the old ache of my rejection at his hands, the coffin-dark, thought-killing grief which had left me thrashing on my bed at night unable to breathe the world without him.

It was then that I remembered the Count's "strange, doubled knowledge" of the French Revolution. Fixing on the idea—it steadied me against the contention—I flung on my dressing gown and raced out into the castle in search of Charlotte and Mireille. I shouted their names but could find them nowhere, and the echoes of my shouts harried me from empty room to empty room where dead, cobwebbed sticks of furniture poked from the shadows like broken spiders. I descended to the laboratory; the iron door stood ajar and the canoe was gone. I ran back and forth between the gravelly beach and the cavern mouth, frantic as a rabbit over whom a snare has fallen. I staggered against the bust of Napoleon which rested on the wooden table . . . where none had been before!

Napoleon. Emperor, warrior, lover, exile, and—to half my mind—completely unknown.

In an instant I became calm, decided. Had I not, I might have gone mad, but my yogic training held my mind against collapse and ordered it to action. The Count had transmitted one of his daughters: that much was certain. I had seen him less than twelve hours previously and, therefore, either Charlotte or Mireille remained. I could not permit him to complete his operation.

Did I think then of my own circumstance compounded a millionfold, that no one should have the authority to create at a whim a world of vanished husbands, abandoned wives and children who were never born? Or did I act for vengeance' sake, understanding that as Guillaume had been returned to me, so he had once been taken from me, and that the Count—in this case, his salvation—might well have been his murderer? Most assuredly *had been* his murderer! Guillaume would not have left me; I had always guessed some essential wrongness in his death. And had not the Count's transmission of his wife occurred eight months before my first glimpse into the ether? That would put it in December 1904, when Guillaume had exhibited a sudden penchant for gambling, one month before his suicide. Still, I do not believe it was vengeance which moved me. My memories of his death were already fading, taking on the aspect of a sad story told me long ago. Perhaps I acted to protect his renewed existence. My motives, evidenced by frail memory alone, seem as opaque and complex to me now as do the etheric structures.

But I did act.

I threw off my dressing gown and sat down on the gravelly shore, chanting my mantra, elevating my body temperature so that the chill water would not weaken me, and I swam the lake and passed through the narrows into the underground river. The pale branchings of light coursed around me; whenever they touched me I experienced fragmentary visions, dislocations; my concentration lapsed and I thought I might dissolve in the river's black grip, just as the snow-white flies in the cavern mouth had melted between my fingers. At last I crawled out onto the base of the stalagmitic ridge. The Count was high above me in the cage, replacing the crystals.

It had been my intent to sabotage the control cabinet, but now, without hesitation, I crept to the cabinet and engaged the lever which raised the iron staircase back from the cage. Hearing the mechanism whine, the Count sprang for the receding top stair, missed and almost fell. He clung to the bars of the cage, peering down into the shadows where I stood.

"Madame Clauvy!" he called, commanding me.

I did not answer; I stared at the orange lever.

"Madame! Let down the stair!"

I adjusted the settings as he had shown me.

"My God, madame!" He slammed the bars in frustration. "You must let me down!"

I felt a sudden wave of pity for him; he was, after all, only a little man in a striped coat trapped atop an improbable pillar of crystal. As if sensing my change in mood, he began to entreat me.

"Please, madame! The first stage of the operation has been successful! Do you understand?"

My hand trembled on the lever.

Once more he pleaded with me, describing the perfect world he would create if I would let down the stair, less a world than a state of grace with which he would endow mankind.

"No!" I screamed. "You have tunneled a hole into hell with your machine! Nothing good can come of it!"

For a moment he stared down into the white glow, sad, as if seeing there his life's resolution.

"How have I injured you, madame? What has happened?"

"Guillaume! He is alive!"

"Your husband?" There was hope in his voice. He gripped the bars and pressed his face between them, trying to find me among the shadows. "Of course! Yes! And you are worried that he may not survive the next transmission. But, madame, we can assure it! Together we will study the structures and thereby determine the optimal eventuality for you both. . . ."

Anger washed over me, anger at the facility with which he promised to guarantee my happiness, as if it were the merest trifle, and anger at the temptation I felt to give in, to let him make my world for me. I pulled down the lever with both hands; if I had had a sword, I would have driven it through him. But I did not look into the cage. I kept my eyes fixed on the crystal column, on the opaque flickerings rising in it, intensifying.

At that moment Mireille struck me in the side with an iron bar. . . . I did not lose consciousness at first, though the pain burst in me like a firework, but then she struck me again, a glancing blow which sent me headfirst into the cabinet, jamming the time setting a millimeter forward of its original position, and I fell. I do not know what she broke in me: ribs, yes, those she broke, but there is some other thing breaking in me still, giving way, causing a sick throb under my heart. She must have stolen up on me while I was talking with the Count. I should have guessed. . . . Well. It is far too late for "should have" and "I wish."

Of course, I did not realize it was Mireille until I regained consciousness and saw her on the ridgetop, a ponderous figure in a white frock whirling, lifting her arms in balletic postures, pausing with the back of her hand pressed to her forehead in a thespian attitude of grief, whirling off again behind a stalagmite. She flittered between the rocky pillars like a poisoned butterfly, too sickly and heavy for proper flight, crying out. . . . I presumed her deranged, but as my senses cleared I understood that this was some ritual attendant upon her father's death. The cries were words, sonorous, long-voweled, a language much like French, darker though, incantatory.

She pronounced the words with fervor, as if they were the names of gods, and the white light ebbed and flowed over the walls, pulsing to her cadence. Listening to her, I grew dizzy, only half aware, and I beheld again in my mind's eye the fissured plateau on which the castle rested, the pit and the wind-carved monolith: so familiar a place, yet so foreign. I knew no more of its history, its hidden significance, than I had known on first seeing it. But it was only the shadow of another world, I think, a world that once we breathed, whose trace remains within our souls, and here was its last bastion: a crumbling temple in which a forlorn handmaiden bemoaned the final loss of hope. The cavern hollowed around her voice. My vision darkened, the light dwindled to an ember's glow, and the throbbing of my wound made a dim, accompanying music.

When Mireille left the cavern she never glanced at me; her eyes were dull, she stumbled, seeming lost without her sister or any further ritual to perform. I heard the canoe scrape on the stony bank, an oar splash, and since then . . . nothing.

I have propped myself up beside the cabinet so that I can look into the white glow of the ether. Phantoms flicker there, rising half out of the light and vanishing, visible as fiery afterimages. Twice I have seen the winged man whom I first encountered along the underground river, and though he disappeared on both occasions, each disappearance was more reluctant, his shadowy form hanging in the air for long minutes like the ghost of an evil flag. He was powerfully built, his skin black and leathery, and his talons were as hooked as fishermen's knives, yet his forehead was high and noble, his nose aquiline and his mouth wide and resolute: the image of the Count.

Prolonged exposure to the ether, I believe, erodes one's position in the world somewhat, siphons off an essential fraction of oneself, and creates an alter image, almost insubstantial, out of all the potentials it embodies. . . . For the ether is, if it is anything graspable in a word, potential. And now, now that the Count is dead, could not this creature be stealing the necessary grain of existence from the residue of his dispersal? So it seems to me by process of intuition, an intuition of the same quality as that which inspired my solution of the Count's equations. And I wonder if my own death here beside this glowing well, my flesh pervaded by the ether in its distilled and excited state, I wonder if it will not give rise to some lesser demon with which he will once more contend.

"Guillaume," whispered Mme. Clauvy, after a pause. "If you are alive, if you hear me, forgive me as I forgive you. These separate destinies we have enacted—they are twice removed from what should have been. . . . I love you." And then: "I will not yet end the transmission. Perhaps something else will occur to me."

A few minutes later Mme. Clauvy said an Act of Contrition. For the next hours, she slept; occasionally she muttered her husband's name or some other half-articulated word. The horizon pinked, gold and crimson rays crowned the rooftops and a band of sky above the sunrise lightened to a pale blue: a Rubens dollhouse of a sky which framed the tower in stately billows of cumulus lacking only cherubim with trumpets and sacred scrolls. . . . Rifle fire intensified along the boulevard des Invalides.

The soldiers on the Champ de Mars drank coffee and watched the streets from their fortifications. Their radios were silent, all commercial stations having gone off the air during the night and the military bands having been judged unreliable by Colonel Chalandon. They were loyal, now, only to themselves, isolated, a nation in the heart of Paris ruled by a dying queen. They spoke infrequently, but when they did their talk was of the three warring generals in Quercy.

"Trinquier will win," said one. "We should be prepared." He was sweating, nervous, shifting his rifle from window to window.

The man beside him laughed. "It might be better if Cadoudal won! Then the world would be full of sissies, no overpopulation, no famine . . . How about it, Goubard? We'll get married after the battle and raise radishes!"

"Hey, what's it matter?" asked a third man. "Trinquier, Cadoudal, Massu . . . We'll wake up in somebody's half-baked dream of paradise, that's for sure!"

At seven twenty-three Mme. Clauvy cried out, "Oh, God!" in a choked voice, and there was a scraping sound, as of fingernails upon a metal surface. The hiss diminished over the next minute, and as it died the tower rippled, a mirage of one hundred years' duration coming to an end; the girders drifted apart, fading, seeming to bend into wavering gray curves, floating up and rearranging into an immense, smoky character—half labyrinth, half rune—which whirled slowly around and faded utterly in that image, leaving an unblemished central expanse of pale-blue sky from which white puffs of cloud were rushing away in opposite directions.

Some of the soldiers knelt, wondering more at this great signal's ending than they had at its inception, and some told their beads for the soul of Mme. Clauvy . . . and for their own: they recognized the fragility of their new world. Others kept their eyes on the streets, rifles pointed, holding to duty. And as the sky deepened further to a cornflower blue and the sun began to strike glints along the roof peaks of the Hôpital des Invalides, the gunfire from the boulevard beyond abruptly died and the air-raid siren atop the Renault building sounded a long, rising note like the howling of a dog, then was switched off.

I believe I am a sucker for stories about alien circuses, but that is not the only reason I admire this story. Kristi Olesen is a writer of controlled power: it crackles in every line. What a vivid, noisy, odorous world she has created in this little space!

BEAST AND BEAUTY

BY KRISTI OLESEN

Kjenla is unique. Watch her! See how my sister uses the trapeze, keeping her wings hidden, dazzling the audience with her color changes! She swings up and up, vaulting for the high curved silver of the ceiling; waves and bursts of gold, orange, ocher and bronze chase and whirl over her slim naked torso; they eddy and recede on her cheeks like blushes gone mad. Look, look! At the apex of her pendulum she releases the bar and somersaults, now a tight ball, pure scarlet, as fiery as her streaming hair, almost too bright to watch.

But where is her catcher? Where is her net? The audience gasps. As one, breath held, they stand, leaning forward as if to reach for her, to pull her to them, to save her. A child screams and is shushed. With a squeal and a thud, someone in the upper tier faints.

A moment of utter silence.

Too fast to follow, she unfurls her wings, the shimmering blue-green triangles between which Kjenla is a gaudy midget. The wings beat, stretch and, wonder of wonders, they catch the air and loft her, and she changes again as she soars over the crowd, her skin now pulsating molten gold. Still the crowd is voiceless, awestruck.

Then, like growing wind, the applause rolls up the aisles, over the packed rows—the stamping, the clapping, the shouting; the audience is wild, shaking the very dome, rattling the concession stands, pounding the clowns into unnoticed antics. Kjenla circles, swoops and angles down to a perfect landing center-ring, letting her wings furl softly about her so that she is gowned in their glimmer. She is magnificent. My pride is more than that of an older sister. Kjenla is part of me. Her perfection is part of me.

The cheering continues as, without taking a bow, she walks slowly into the tunnel from which the next act pours. Still the crowd calls for more, ignoring the new entertainment, a six-legged beast and its two-legged trainer who both caper foolishly, begging attention. But Kjenla does not return. Gradually the crowd quiets. Kjenla will not go back for an encore. She never does.

She comes to me. She is drained, shaking, her colors fading to tan, her expression slack and unfocused.

I take her to her tent. It is the largest in the enclosure, as it should be to house a star like my sister. It is of the same fabric as the big globe and it shines, a silver beacon standing separate from the lesser dwellings of lesser performers. She has a private tent because she is a virgin and must stay so, or she will be distracted from her work. I see to her purity. I let no one close to her. She obeys me.

Kjenla has been with Astounding Interalien Entertainments for only a year, Chamel time, but already she is their headliner and their biggest draw. Word of her artistry runs before us. The shows are sold out far in advance. On each world we visit, a crowd waits to see her disembark; they chant Kjenla's name, stretching and jostling to catch a glimpse of her. Perhaps they are disappointed, then, to find only a slight, caped and hooded figure walking quickly past. But after the show, not one leaves the big globe feeling cheated. My sister never fails to astonish.

On our home world, Chamel, they taunted us, assaulted us, burned our home, and drove Mother to suicide. And the ignorant ground-crawlers of Chamel are not unusual; the bounders of any world would deal us the same misery if we tried to live among them, but as long as we're part of this circus they can adore us. We are in our place, safely ensconced with the other crossbreeds, freaks and mutants. From the moment the bounders enter the Interalien enclosure, giggling at the chill of the force field that shivers between its silver posts and wires, they know they are in an alien world—our world. As they walk the worn purple carpet leading to the big globe, their titillation is increased by a display of garish tri-dee posters showing the headliners, each more impossibly colored than the last, and all much larger than life. Interalien has managed to make even my gentle sister look fearsome, giving her pointed teeth and wicked talons. But this is what the bounders pay for. They want to forget the blandness of their lives; we give them danger in careful doses and a chance to laugh too hard.

So Kjenla flies while the audience gapes, and when she lands I take over.

I towel away her sweat, then oil and scrape her, treating her fragile and precious skin tenderly. I must attend to this for her. Left to her own devices, she would not take proper care of herself. Her talents do not include a sound grasp of day-to-day necessities.

Next I spray her limp wings with a steeped herb brew of my own concoction. I help her into the night sheath that I wove and stitched of her own scarlet hair; I let nothing harsh or foreign touch her. I also weave for the others in our company who must wear special fabrics, but what I make for Kjenla takes precedence. My labor is better spent on a true artist.

And I make her skin oil, pressing it from seeds which I gather on Chamel, as I gather and prepare all her food. Kjenla is a fussy eater. She says her belly is too nervous to handle the local trash; most of it is unsuited to our metabolism anyway. With the amount of nugget Interalien pays us, we can afford to eat the very best. But she will not eat this evening. To fly, she must be nothing but bright skin and hollow bone, and her body cannot be distracted by digestion while she sleeps. Kjenla must have her rest or she won't perform at peak. I make certain she shows to her best advantage.

The Sculptor was fueling his whip, brow ribbed in concentration. Taking care not to spill the flammable liquid, he filled the reservoir in the whip's handle, then checked the explosive charges in the tip. The first crack of the whip would pump the fuel and set off blasts that did the actual carving. Oxygen rushing over the strap excited the fuel, increasing the heat. This was his favorite moment in the performance. The bounders never failed to shriek when the sparks flew.

He sat between two brittle stones; he would chose one of them to carve for the audience this evening; it didn't really matter which. The Sculptor did not believe in muses and cared nothing for inspiration. Mysterious forms lying hidden in stone? Nonsense. Why give the credit to a ghost? His was the work, his the idea; he was solely responsible for his success. He didn't ponder his creations once they were finished; the act of carving itself was what he enjoyed. After each performance he left the jagged, soot-contoured sculpture where it stood. He had no further use for it; he could always make another. He fancied the carvings appropriate monuments to show common folk that the Sculptor had once passed through. It gave the bounders a little thrill.

Solid stone and concrete pleasure: these were the finest parts of life. He rubbed his crotch, thinking of pleasure. The problem with being so famous was that females were afraid to approach you. And the problem with Interalien was that it never stayed on one planet long enough for the females to lose their shyness. The Sculptor never got as much as he wanted.

Kjenla. There was a pretty name. He put the whip down and strode to his tent flap. Clouds were piling in the east. He stretched, yawned and rubbed the stubble on his chin. Yellow light fell from the door of Kjenla's tent.

Now she slumbers, curved lips slightly parted, her breathing even, skin pale, pulsating mild umber. She has time to rest, but I must go back to my work—the stitching of costumes, both repairs and construction. I unroll a bolt of fabric, smooth the wrinkles, then grip my shears and run them over the whetstone again and again until they are honed to a perfect edge. They glisten in

my hand, warm. I make the first cut. I need no pattern. I know
Kjenla's body better than my own.

How lucky that my fingers are clever, even if my color-changes
are foolish. "Ren," Kjenla had said to me when, as a child, I'd
been taunted once more by the other youngsters for my lack of
color control, "don't listen to them. They're foolish babies.
They're jealous. You can do things they can't. You got Father's
hands. Not one of those brats can paint or write, or make things
the way you do. I wish I'd gotten his hands too, instead of these
stupid wings. They're always in my way." Here she rustled them
in annoyance. "They have no use at all. What good are wings if
you can't fly?"

This was one of the few times when she comforted me, though
my untamed changing gave me more than my share of humilia-
tion and I could have used her support. Usually I held and
soothed her, sopping up her tears, assisting in her vain attempts
at flight. Wings were no good at all in the thick gravity of
Chamel; she could barely make them flutter. But in the low-gee
of the Interalien Entertainment's big globe, as she rides the air
currents that pucker and flatten the sleek silver fabric between
the triangular struts of the dome, there Kjenla is the best of both
Father and Mother; she makes good their mistakes.

While I sew, I sit at the tent's flap to catch the night breeze,
odd-smelling like the breezes on all the foreign worlds we play.
I'm not even certain what this planet is called—begins with some
unpronounceable guttural, I believe. They're the same to me, the
languages and the alien forms, as insubstantial as a male's love
and as unimportant. I see only Kjenla clearly, care only about my
little sister, the crossbreed flyer. Perhaps I worry about her too
much. She can be stubborn, and she clings tenaciously to her
fancies. I spend more time than I should in keeping her energy
channeled into her art. I must quell her recent tendency to respond to the advances of certain males. I have no idea what she
sees in them. Sometimes I am frustrated by her artlessness.

Ouch! I've pricked my finger, and the blood makes a dark blue
dot on the cloth. Dark blue, like Father the flyer, grounded on
Chamel by an alien wife and two half-breed children. My restless

father, always reminiscing about the small world he came from,
about ruddy light washing down from a huge red sun, about
soaring easily from treetop to massive black treetop, always re-
calling the past while Mother listened sympathetically, praying
he would stay until the children were grown.

He didn't. Kjenla was hardly more than a baby when he reacti-
vated his contract with the Conglom, signed on a passing
freighter and took off for worlds where his wings could carry
him. He vowed to return, but of course he never did; he was
untrustworthy and inconstant, as are all of his sex.

Father is never spoken of between us, though once Kjenla did
say that she remembered him. She is confused. She was too
young. What she recalls of him must be what Mother told her,
and Mother never spoke against him. She was generous and for-
giving to all, as kind to the sadistic bounders who finally caused
her death as she was to strays like Father or to her own strange-
looking daughters. Mother was as artless as Kjenla has come to
be.

Arno is approaching. He is a suitor, one of many who pay
effusive and unending court to my sister, haunt her by day and
dream of her by night. If only I could depend on her to discourage them! But this, like so many other chores, is left to me.
Though most of the suitors are impossible pests and some become dangerous when thwarted, Arno is no more than a mild
annoyance. He is unusually thoughtful and intelligent for a male.
Were his method of communication not accompanied by such an
alarming succession of stinks, I might find him a rather pleasant
companion. At least he has not brought his familiars with him
this evening. I find them most annoying.

"Good evening, Lady Ren. Pleasant little world this, eh?" He
stands politely downwind, but still a smell like freshly dropped
feces assails me. It is by these emanations that he communicates
with his familiars. I must not gag. I treat all the suitors with as
much consideration as I can muster; better pass the time with
Arno than any of the others. At least I know he won't attack me
or try to sneak into the tent behind my back. He is not like that
sculptor.

In a way, Arno's talent is akin to Kjenla's. He, too, executes changes, though his medium is not entirely intrinsic, as is my sister's. He uses his familiars, hundreds of insects whose tiny crystalline bodies shatter simple white light into ever-changing patterns. They dart about him, a prismatic cloud, and in response to his pungent commands they create flickering images, half finished and blending. In me, these pictures evoke equally half-completed emotions, partial memories. I find his work quite stimulating, if sadly nostalgic and a bit frustrating. I don't know what Kjenla thinks of his patterns, for she never speaks of any art but her own.

Arno takes my silence for disgust at his most recent aroma; his distress only intensifies the odor, bringing it to the level of sun-rotted flesh. I gasp, almost unable to contain my nausea. Smiling, I master my reaction, hoping he hasn't taken offense.

"I really don't notice new worlds, Master Arno." I am still smiling, trying not to breathe. Abruptly, I change color radically until I am mottled with deepest purple, an unheard-of shade for a changer. Arno is trying not to notice. He is as polite as I.

I pause until I'm certain the change is over. When I continue, I am even more formal. I do not want to share embarrassments with him. He must not become too familiar.

"If you're here to see Kjenla, I must tell you she is indisposed. Her performance was particularly trying this evening."

"And particularly magnificent. What beauty! It is rapture to watch her, rapture!" For a moment, thoughts of Kjenla seem to lessen, even sweeten, his stench. I get in two or three deep breaths. His pods bunch. He is preparing to sit.

"I'm sorry, Master Arno," I say crisply enough to brook no argument. "Kjenla will not wake for many hours. You can't wait for her. Try tomorrow afternoon, after the matinee. If she's not too tired, I'll let you speak with her."

He nods in resignation, emits a particularly vile blast and wanders off, pods compressing and springing in the peculiar canter that lets one distinguish a romper from other aliens even at a distance. It's too bad about his smells. Away from his familiars he should be able to withhold the odors, but, like me, he lacks control. If not for that, he might have returned home from his stint with our circus as a respected artist. He could have spent his old age a famous professor, teaching romper youths how to guide their own familiars in light displays of depth and originality. Unhappily, they ridicule him; so he is rootless, a lifelong stranger, as I am. As is my sister.

Kjenla stirs in her sleep. I must go to her, for she never dreams well unless I cradle her, laying my stocky body next to her tender one, petting away her agitation with my nimble fingers. Sometimes she tries to respond to the fondling, but I stop her. She is pristine and I will keep her so. She is special: she has pleasures only I will ever understand, and she must be satisfied with this, for the mundane relations between sexes would only confuse her. I will not have her distracted.

So Arno hadn't been able to get in to see Kjenla either! The Sculptor was glad to discover he wasn't the only spurned suitor. He watched as Arno wandered disconsolately through the stage door into the big globe. What a stupid creature that rounder was, with its rubbery foot-things and no face worth calling a face. The Sculptor charmed himself with a vision of crushing Arno's skull, or slicing at those fleshy rolls of alien belly with a few well-placed lashes of the whip. A living body to carve! He scratched lingeringly over his palm, imagining. No, stone was better, less messy; touching that creature would only degrade a great artist.

How had he, the Sculptor, the finest hotwhip rock carver in the galaxy (perhaps the universe?), ended up in this zoo full of freaks and half-breeds?

The answer, he had to admit, was simple. Nugget. Lots of nugget. And heated fantasies featuring Kjenla made the days more interesting. Yes, she was a freak too, but really, such a beauty shouldn't go to waste. And no one else should have her. Alien or no, she was special. Such a tiny, frail girl, yet when she flew she was as powerful and as fascinating as the Sculptor's whip. Even away from her trapeze, she held herself in a way that gave the lie to the apparent weakness of her body.

Once, as he watched the exhausted Kjenla join her sister Ren in the tunnel after a performance, the Sculptor had witnessed a sharp exchange between the two females. He had no idea what they had quarreled over, but anger soon banished the tiredness in Kjenla and she stood straight; the sight of the little female mustering such strength after so draining a performance had forced prickling tears to the Sculptor's eyes.

He rubbed his thumb roughly over his chin. That picture of Kjenla, standing proud and angry, defying her sister, was firmly impressed on the Sculptor's senses and he enjoyed replaying it despite the tug of embarrassment he felt at his own momentary weakness. He had seen an intimacy, and now he felt he understood Kjenla. No matter how often Ren told tales to the contrary, the beautiful flyer was not so breakable—so spineless.

She couldn't hide behind that ugly sister forever. He snorted, thinking of wide Ren with her unpleasant manner and her habit of flushing muddily at odd moments. She had a good spiel, that dumpy older sister—lots of bravado—but they both knew she was no match for his physical strength. He would put up with those frigid noes just so long. He would have Kjenla eventually, tonight better than tomorrow. Perhaps the time for a frontal attack had come? Yes. Yes indeed.

He hefted his whip as he would flex a limber muscle, enjoying the feel of the grip. Snap! The whip arced above his head, blue sparks flying, the strap burning with yellow flame from haft to tip, its heat distorting the air about it, highlighting the Sculptor's hair with gold. He smiled, his neat white teeth transmuted to metal, returning the whip's glow.

I keep my eyes shut. I know the footsteps, unusually light for such a large male, even gentler now as he tries to slide past me, believing I am asleep. Kjenla is awake as well, for her skin is warming, her muscles no longer lax. I will let this encounter run a partial course. Kjenla, my sweet, naïve Kjenla, may lose me someday. I must hold myself in check to let her experience the evil in men for herself. She is simple, but not stupid. He will be so crude that even Kjenla will notice it. She cannot help but be repelled by this brute of a rock chopper.

I peep through slitted lids and see the Sculptor's massive shadow hulk black, cast on the tent wall by the luster of the night-light near the door. Almost to the bed, he pauses. When still, he is uncannily like one of his sculptures: a shape frozen in the possibility of motion. Though they are usually abstracts with little relation to anything living, the shapes he carves are jagged and ponderous, as he is, and they all have this quality of static potential, as if each were an elemental force waiting for the right catalyst. That catalyst will not be my sister.

He moves again and I can smell him. He has just washed himself, but the harshest soap cannot scrape away his own hot scent, like beaten iron and hard scorched earth.

Kjenla sits up, blinking. Her hair is tousled; she is lovely.

"Kjenla?" he whispers, kneeling at the bedside. "Are you angry that I've come to see you so late? I've wanted so much to see you—to speak with you." His words are tender. He leaks sincerity. My sister makes a small noise, like a covered animal. I try to gauge her expression, but her face is in shadow.

The Sculptor expels his breath and it brushes over my arm, warm but oddly dry. "Has your sister told you when I've come before? I have. Many times. But she always turns me away." Only a shade of bitterness; he plays the martyr with fine polish.

Kjenla begins to speak, stops, then glances over her shoulder at me. Her skin is a pleasant rose edged in crimson, and her hair toys with the light, flaring and subsiding. She looks puzzled and a little sad. She turns back to the Sculptor, who leans forward.

"Did you say something?" he says. He moves closer, not yet making the mistake of trying to caress her.

"I *have* heard you speak to my sister." Her voice cracks, stiff with sleep. "But you shouldn't be here. Ren will be furious if she wakes. I can't imagine why she hasn't already. Usually she sleeps so lightly. She wakes every time I turn. I—"

He puts his hand on the coverlet and Kjenla shrinks back, but not enough. She appears coy. Will she never learn? Does she think she can control him? He is a master of this game, and she cannot help but lose to him.

"I won't disturb her," he says, then: "Do you care for me, Kjenla? You must know that I want you. I want you to be mine." She is staring at his hand. He places the other next to it, and they both gaze down, bashful as children. His duplicity sickens me. I find I am tense, breathing rapidly.

Kjenla looks at her own hands, then back at his. "I—I've noticed you often, in the big globe. You are an artist. Your whip is a living thing. I—I've seen it in my dreams. And your work is strong—it's—clean, and graceful. Like your hands. The work shows well on them. Mine are so weak and silly—"

"No!" His whisper is crisp. Had I been sleeping, I'd surely have wakened at the noise. But Kjenla no longer seems to care how loud her suitor becomes. "You're stronger than you know," he continues. "Your sister tries to make you weak, but she has no real power over you. Do you want me? Do you?"

He waits for an answer, wide chest inches from her thin form, full lips ready to smile. He is confident.

This is not right. She shifts closer to him, and their arms touch. She is not put off. She is intrigued. Can it be possible that she is taken in by this crass male? I have overestimated my sister. She will not have the chance to respond any further.

As I sit up, my hand closes on the shears, which I keep next to the bed, long blades sharp as crystal. I shout, waving them before his startled face.

"Get out! Out! I'll cut you to scraps! You dare enter Kjenla's tent at night! Thief! Robber!" I am screaming. The Sculptor is frozen, deciding whether to attack, ignore or disappear. I keep screaming and hear the patter of running outside, anxious voices chattering closer. The Sculptor hears it too. He is not deep, but he is quick. With one longing glance at Kjenla, he is on his feet, agilely dodging out the door, not to be caught at the scene of his intended crime.

Kjenla is startled, her back rigid, eyes hard. Is she angry with me? No matter. I will calm her as I always do. She is entirely dependent upon me.

I go outside to make explanations to the knot of curious performers gathered before the door. When Kjenla is cooler we will talk of this and I will have her understand, though this may take some time.

And I will take action against the Sculptor, who is now an active threat—a threat I shall remove. Kjenla is a complete innocent. She does not even know what coupling is. She never will. The Sculptor will never again plague my sister.

Arno's tent was filled with scents and the whining of his familiars. At breakfast, he had overheard a couple of performers snickering about the Sculptor's attempt on Kjenla. He had been unable to swallow his food, and knew his odor must be foul.

In his shelter, where he wouldn't offend the others, he let his smells heighten and lessen, changing from bitter to cloying to tangy to grotesque. The familiars swarmed about him, disturbed. At this time of day they should have been collecting the secretions from Arno's skin and hurrying to deposit them in their hive, but he wouldn't let the whirling insects settle. He wanted them hungry. He needed them angry, dangerous, edgily ready to do as he bade. This was risky, as his familiars could deliver a vicious, if tiny, bite. Normally they were docile and easily handled, but when frightened they were unpredictable. Arno would chance it. He felt he had enough control, and he wanted them mean.

He tried to relax among them, ignoring their insistent buzz and planning again what he would do to the Sculptor—what his familiars would do.

The matinee would be crowded. The Sculptor would stride center-ring, whip in hand, and the stone would be there waiting for him, an angular monolith. Arno would be in the tunnel surrounded by his familiars, as usual. Maybe he would let the Sculptor give one last stroke of the flamed whip. Yes, that would be fitting.

Then Arno would release his insects: impatient, hungry, infuriated. They would rend the mass that was the Sculptor to nothing. Maybe the rock carver would run, vainly swatting at the swarm, shrieking. It would do no good. They would leave his bare bones in a pile, center-ring. What a show! The bounders would ogle and screech, thinking this an innovative if sordid entertainment. The Sculptor would pay for his violation of Kjenla with the nuggets of blood that would splatter the ring.

Arno batted at the familiars who were trying to rest on his pods. He emitted an odor akin to burning hair, pungent enough to sting human eyes. His familiars hummed maniacally. They were almost ready.

Kjenla is more furious with me than she has ever been before. She will not speak, except to whine about trivialities, and she will not leave her bed. I've told Interalien management she is ill and cannot perform the matinee. It is best this way. It is better that she will not see what happens to her suitor. She is sensitive and I shield her from all violence. Her feelings must come first.

How she glares at me! I've never seen her hold a mood so long. I must not let her distract me. I have to finish the garment in time to have it delivered to the Sculptor just before the matinee. He is hard on his costumes; he uses two or three a week, giving the company seamstresses more work than any other performer. Proud fool that he is, he will wear this new suit, never wondering where it came from. He does not heed details. He will be pleased at how well he looks in it, and enjoy the way the cut and color set off his physique. He will put it on without a second thought.

The matinee will be crowded. The Sculptor will stride center-ring, whip in hand, and the stone will be there waiting for him, an angular monolith. I won't watch; I am not sadistic.

I will be satisfied by the screams when, as he unleashes that whip and the first flames leap out, sparks bursting, the garment I have made—the special fabric I have used—ignites in glorious, unquenchable flame. A hungry bonfire, it will consume him entire while the bounders behold in astonishment, thinking this a fine bit of magic. Their applause, as the smoke filters to the ceiling, will be the Sculptor's last ovation.

Gradually Kjenla will come to accept the fitness of this deed, and one day she will thank me. Or she will discover a new trick on the trapeze and she will forget the Sculptor forever. This is my sister: always an artist, living within her art. She can be a burden,

but I am her only source of protection and consolation. I will ·
never lose her love.

Arno waited in the tunnel, Ren at the main entrance, as the
audience filed past the mutants' booths and entered the big globe.
They waited through the opening acts, Suliman and his Shape
Shifters, Largo of the Rubber Face. The Sculptor's slot was first
after intermission. His costume was ready for him in the dressing
room.

Arno's familiars were ravenous as they circled the romper, not
allowed to alight.

The bounders settled back into their seats after intermission,
impatient and noisy. Arno shuffled nervously, wondering
whether the insects would remain in his control. The Sculptor
would have to pass Arno to get into the ring. He was late. The
audience began to grumble, shouting for the show to start; they
stamped rhythmically, and the seats shook in time. Still no Sculptor. Arno grew more uneasy. The rock carver was rarely late and
never, no matter how ill, missed his slot altogether. Another act
had to be sent in to take his place: three blue-scaled, long-fanged
snaky creatures, whose trainer prodded them into violent mock
battles. They hissed, reared and spat as the trainer's goad pricked
in and out, driving them to frenzy. The audience crowed, delighted.

Arno hesitated in his lively cloud. Assuming the Sculptor
wasn't paralyzed or dead, the only motivation strong enough to
keep him from hacking at his stones was—Arno began to tremble. He wavered, nerves pulled to breaking, then dashed for
Kjenla's tent. He spotted Ren on his way out; no questions or
answers passed between them. They ran side by side, the familiars straggling behind. The romper and the changer raced
through the tent's door together.

The bedclothes were scrambled, the night table tipped, and the
rock carver's body was humped gracelessly on the floor,
facedown, crimson leaking from him.

Kjenla was pinioned under his bulk, one wing outspread, angled uncomfortably and covered with blood. Her eyes were shut

and she was an unpleasant beige, backed with blue. Ren sped to
her side, skin garish with blotched and streaking color-changes.
Kjenla tried weakly to move her head; it was wedged under the
Sculptor's shoulder. Ren put out her hand, hesitated, then
brushed a blood-stiffened hair from Kjenla's cheek.

"Kjenla . . . sister. Are you hurt? Did he hurt you?" Ren
was shaking, her forehead violet, clenched fists green. "What did
he do to you? Did you let him . . . how far did he . . . what
has happened?" She leaned to push at the corpse but could not
budge it. She shook her head, incredulous. "Kjenla?" she said
again, sitting back on her heels. Arno shifted uneasily in the
doorway. Finally Kjenla spoke, her words little more than a sigh.

"He was bruising me."

Then she fell asleep.

I hold the scissors. The blades glint at me through drying
blood. Arno hangs uselessly at my shoulder, hopping from pod to
pod and looking distraught. I wish he would leave.

Kjenla will be sore, but she is intact. Weeks will pass before she
can use her color changes properly again, and months before she
will fly. Her left wing is torn. It took all the combined strength of
Arno and me to rescue her—to lift the corpse and free my sister.
It must have been horrible for her, suffocating under such a
weight, not certain whether it was corpse or man, struggling to
escape, but this was her own fault. She did not heed my warn-
ings.

I won't wake her. She needs her rest. Tomorrow I will make
certain she understands her error.

The stab wound is deep. The shears went between the ribs into
the heart, and the blood is everywhere, congealing. His eyes are
wide and his mouth open. He was surprised. He called himself an
artist, one of a kind, yet could not understand Kjenla's singular-
ity or her obsession. He dealt with her as he would with a young
girl or a pet. Innocence is not the same as childishness. He took
curiosity for encouragement.

I am not proud of Kjenla. Though she did, in the end, defend
what was most important, there was no excuse for her foolishness

in welcoming a male into her tent. Did she feign her illness in order to tryst with that rock carver? I hope not. I will find out. If I am to continue in my role as her protector, she must never lie to me.

I hold myself partly responsible. I should have talked longer to her, given her more convincing explanations, seen how intense was her fury at me, reminded her more often about what Father did to Mother and how Mother died, shown her that all males are alien to us—all males, always.

Arno stoops over Kjenla and reaches to finger her lovely forehead. His familiars dance frantically; his smell is hideous. I leap forward and pull him back from her.

"No, Arno, no! Can't you see she's sleeping? Don't disturb her. You'd better leave. She needs me and only me. Please, Arno, do not intrude. You must go."

He begins to reply and stops. I glance at him, and in his face I see the Sculptor's huge shadow, the unending threat. The noise of the familiars grows louder; they seem to be trying to entice him to leave. Finally, stiffly, unwillingly, he goes. I can see by the set of his retreating shoulders that he has not given up. His fascination with Kjenla has rooted deeply.

That is too bad. I like Arno. But I never make the same mistake twice where Kjenla is concerned. I'm ashamed of myself for having been deceived once.

I straighten the blankets and lift her gently to the bed. I will wash the blood off later, when she wakes. As I bathe her, I'll tell her tales meant for children and I will sing for her and hold her close when she cries. We will talk about the Sculptor. I will not let her forget. If Arno calls tomorrow, I will send him away. I hope for his sake that he decides to abandon this prize, the beautiful half-breed flyer.

Yes. Yes; tomorrow, as I wash away the blood, I will use today's trauma to remind Kjenla how much she depends upon me. She will be confused. She will be frightened and desperate for guidance. She is accustomed to my touch, and it soothes her.

When she reaches for help, she will find me. She is my sister. She is unique. We are freaks, and the only place we have is the one we make together. She will never leave me. I am the only one who can give her what she needs.

What I look for at Clarion when I am trying to guess which students will become famous is prolific talent. There is no way you are not going to see more of Nina Hoffman, unless God zaps her with a lightning bolt tomorrow morning.

LOST LIVES

BY NINA KIRIKI HOFFMAN

Out of the grass a gleam of light called to him. It appeared to be a locket.

Tom, who spent a lot of time looking at the ground, stooped to pick it up. He had found quarters and once a watch which hadn't worked. He had enjoyed taking it apart. Tiny gears, intricate and perfect, seemed to Tom like the inner workings of centipedes, what you might find if you dared unsprong a frog.

In his hand the gleam muted, shadowed from the sun. Out of its radiance a shape emerged, a rounded heart the size of a dove's egg. Tom searched for the catch that would halve the heart and show him its insides. Pictures, branches off somebody's family tree, he thought. No button or knob disturbed the surface of the heart. It reminded him of his grandmother's thumb knuckle, worried like a walnut. He closed his hand on the heart. It pulsed in his fist, warm and spooky. He put it in his pocket to join flints, bottle caps and marbles. It made a warm spot against his thigh. He felt a little afraid of it. He ran away from the ball park and his cousin Rafe, trailing sunlight and grass scent like the tail of a kite.

Splashing through puddles of leaf-filtered sun, he scattered footsteps up the sidewalk. Blood pounded, breath pounded, all of him a piston, yet he felt there was some small place at the bottom of his lungs he couldn't reach, couldn't fill with new air. Like

precoughs—none of them convincing until the last deep fire-
works-inside-eyelids cough from the central core that chased the
throat tickles away. Tom ran on past the place he called home
this month, dipping down canyons of streets, then jumping up
curb cliffs, leaping concrete cracks and tree-root bucklings, stray-
ing on fringes of lawn and fragments of wall. He ran out of
houses, emerging at last into a wide-sky place where spiky weeds
rimmed ditches and rusted barbedwires tried to keep the country
from running onto the road.

He stopped at a stile and leaned on it, gulping air, then
climbed it to sit on the top step, letting himself collapse into
himself. Breath burst in and out of him in involuntary waves,
invading even the deepest chambers of his lungs. Real life. He
had to run so hard to find it. Sweat beaded on his face. He could
feel trickles down his back.

He leaned to unbend his pocket, then reached in, found the
heart by its shape and warmth, and pulled it out into the sun.

The sweat from his palm sheathed it in shine. He turned it over
with his forefinger, looking for any sign that it had once been a
pendant. A girl wouldn't wear this around her neck. It was too
big and too ugly. Maybe it was a nugget. But it was too symmet-
rical to be natural.

It was warm.

It made his hand tingle.

He closed his fingers around it again, closed his eyes, closed
out sounds and scents and focused on the feeling in his left hand,
ignoring the breeze cooling him as it stole his sweat, ignoring the
sun beating down on his head. His fingertips had folded to touch
the heel of his hand. Inside that small-boned cage he felt pulsing
warmth, rhythmic as the beat of his heart. Tom began to feel
sleepy.

The tingle shot up his arm, jabbed his shoulder. He jerked and
dropped the heart, picking up splinters in the seat of his pants,
opening his eyes to sun glare too bright to see through.

Pain. It could give him pain. Tom squinted until the colors
seeped back into things. Then he stood up, brushed himself off
and peered into the shadow-cold spot under the stile where the

heart had fallen. If he took it home, Rafe would steal it the way he had stolen everything that gave Tom's past a shape: the little silver-framed picture of Mother; the coiled silver snake ring his father had left him; the single crack-cornered snapshot showing three people together. An aunt had told Tom he was the baby in the picture.

He saw a gleam under the stile. He took off his T-shirt, wrapped it around his hand and reached between steps to grab the heart. Solid. Heavy. He transferred it to his pocket, then pulled his shirt on again. Sun too often burned his skin to redness; tanning never seemed to take.

He had missed lunch. Aunt Rosemary wouldn't care. She rarely policed him the way other aunts had. Saturday afternoon, Tom thought, walking back toward town, Nostalgia Theatre; she would be watching some old black-and-white movie from the thirties with lots of talk and little action.

Where would Cousin Rafe be? Back from ball practice yet? Wondering where Tom had gone when he ran off? Tom felt a grin grow from the inside out. Old Rafe. Tom felt like a wavery reflection every time he looked at Rafe, who had Tom's features intensified into handsome. Wonder-boy Rafe, kind Rafe, good Rafe, who had listened to every story Tom told about his past and who got so much pleasure out of taking Tom with him everywhere. Rafe had given Tom a new nickname: Shadow. The more time Tom spent with Rafe, the less substantial he felt. Today Tom had run away for the first time.

He walked back into the shadows of the town, retraced the trail that had carried him away. This time he stopped in front of "home." He let himself in through the chain-link fence gate, followed flagstones across the shaded lawn, climbed the front-porch steps and stopped for a moment to look back. Little night lived on his aunt's street. Trees spread branches above the asphalt to keep the sky out. When Tom had arrived a month ago, he had thought he would like it. A quiet street, people who stayed to themselves, giving each other glimpses of their lives, just enough to build curiosity and speculation, no more. Life in a forest. But Rafe kept taking him away, out into the sunlight. Bike rides.

Swimming. Baseball. Places where Rafe could shine and Tom couldn't.

He turned his back to the street, crossed the porch and opened the screen door to let himself into the house. TV noise cottoned around him as he passed the door to the living room. He waded through it, then on past the staircase. The swinging door flapped once behind him as he entered the kitchen.

Rafe, stocky, tanned and cheery, stared at him with eyes twice the intense blue of the ones Tom saw in mirrors. He held a dew-beaded glass of frothy milk in his hand. He looked like a commercial. "Shadow!" he said. "Where the heck did you disappear to? I was starting to worry."

"Oh, I just—I found . . ." He reached into his pocket, thinking. He had had to concentrate really hard for it to hurt him last time; if he just touched it a second he would still be safe. But he was wrong. Webs of tingling spun up his arm, past his shoulder this time, up his neck, into his head.

—My name is Hannah.

The momentary freeze of all Tom's muscles thawed again. He managed to pull his hand out of his pocket.

"What? What'd you find?" Rafe put down his milk and surged forward, looking less like a milk commercial and more like the malt liquor bull. "I saw you stoop for something before you took off. What was it?"

"That?" Her name was Hannah. "It was just an old button." Rafe might break her if she hurt him the way she had hurt Tom. "But I ripped my pants when I bent over. I had to run home and sew them up."

"Where? Where is this rip?" Rafe took Tom's shoulder and turned him around.

The jeans, like everything Tom owned, were old. He pointed to the newest string of stitches.

"What have you got in your pocket?" Rafe asked.

Damn.

—Hide, Hannah, he thought, and dug down into his pocket. He pulled out all the nonwarm things he could grasp, then dumped them all on the white-topped kitchen table. Three rocks.

Two marbles. A couple of bottle caps with letters inside. The beady chain from the bathtub plug. A quarter, a nickel and a button.

Rafe grabbed the money and pounced on the button before Tom got a proper look at it. He couldn't remember picking it up. He didn't much care. The warmth of the heart still touched his thigh.

"It's pretty," said Rafe, holding the button up. Light bent amber through the button's translucence. Rafe put it in his pocket. "Better clean up before Mom comes in for another glass of wine," said Rafe, waving at Tom's pile of things on the table. Tom refilled his pocket. "She left you a sandwich in the fridge. Want to go roller-skating?"

"I don't—"

"You don't, huh? Feel yourself getting shadowy? You feel like moving on again, hey? Want me to talk to Mom?" Rafe laughed. He drained the glass of milk, then set it in the sink and ran water in it. "You come to the pool with me tomorrow afternoon, Shadow."

"I will."

Rafe laughed again and left through the swinging door. Tom felt like throwing dishes. Like taking an ax to the kitchen table. Like hitting Rafe in the stomach with a bowling ball. He had been bounced from one set of relatives to another too many times. He was running out of new sets. He really liked Aunt Rosemary, and she seemed to like him. Rafe could spoil it all. Rafe loved knowing he could spoil it all.

Tom went to the refrigerator and got out the plastic-wrapped sandwich and the milk carton. He was pouring a glass of milk when his aunt wandered in and dropped a kiss on his head. "Hi, sweetie."

"Hi. Thanks for lunch, Aunt Rosemary," Tom said. She winced. "Sorry. Rose," he said, and watched for her answering smile. It came. He relaxed. He had to start getting that right! She might be like the others and lose patience.

"I'm sorry too, sweetie. I know they hammered manners at

you before you got to me. It just makes me feel old before my time. Want to come sit with me? It's Fred Astaire."

He really wanted to go up to his room and try to find out who Hannah was. "Sure," he said, putting away the milk and picking up sandwich and glass. Aunt Rosemary smiled, took the bottle of Lambrusco out of the refrigerator and led the way back to the living room, holding the doors for Tom so he wouldn't have to elbow them aside.

They watched quietly until the next commercial. She pressed the mute button on the remote control and looked at Tom in the sudden silence. "I like you so much, Tommy," she said. "You're very like your father. Rafe isn't a bit like his father was, and I don't think he's like me either. Sometimes I feel I don't know him. Is he mean to you?"

Half of him thought his chance had come. The other half told him this was a trap. "Aunt—Rose. I—"

Her eyelids lowered. She lit a cigarette, taking a long drag. "So," she said. "I don't know where he gets it. I had pets when he was a baby, a dog and a cat. Never again, Tommy. All the things the relatives said about you, I thought maybe you could hold your own." She glanced at the screen. Fred and Ginger were dancing in an otherwise empty pavilion. "Now I'm not so sure. What does he do?"

Tom thought back over the past month and shook his head. "Nothing. He doesn't do anything." Steal things, maybe, but that seemed less important. "It's all mental junk," he said. "He never does anything that actually hurts, Au— Rose. He only makes me go places where I look stupid."

"Makes you? How does he make you?"

The little warm lump at his hip sent a pulse of tingle through him. Static seemed to swarm through the hairs on the back of his head. Tom looked up and around. Rafe was standing in the door to the front hall.

"Nothing," said Tom.

"What?" She turned. "Rafe?"

"Mom? Having a nice chat? I just came down to find out what time supper is. Maybe you should cook something fattening.

Shadow needs more meat on his bones. I don't think he's eating enough. Sometimes I think he hallucinates." Rafe stepped forward into the light so that they could see his confident, pitying smile. Tom admired Rafe's sense of theater for the eighteenth time. Imagine knowing how the light would fall on one's face.

"Supper's at six-thirty, like always. Let's go shopping, Tom. I'll buy you some eclairs."

"All right."

"But, Mom. Your movie," Rafe said.

"I've seen this movie thirty-four times," said Rosemary. She switched the TV off with the remote control, then stubbed out her cigarette and stood up.

"I'll come with you," said Rafe.

"I didn't invite you, dear," she said. She yawned into the back of her hand. "Come, Tom." Picking up the almost-empty bottle of wine, she marched past Rafe and out to the kitchen.

Tom followed as far as the door. Rafe grabbed a handful of the front of his T-shirt and stopped him. "You tell her anything and I'll have her disbelieving it by tomorrow. Scared of you. Wanting to get rid of you."

Outright threats, thought Tom, detached. He's losing his finesse.

"Remember that." Rafe let go of his shirt and shoved him back.

"I will," said Tom.

He and Aunt Rosemary climbed silently into her four-door yellow sedan. She lit a cigarette, started the engine and backed smoothly out of the driveway. Tom leaned into his seat back and closed his eyes. The intensity had faded out of everything. He had come too close to real life; he had almost let it cut him.

Five minutes later he opened his eyes. They should have reached the supermarket by now. Instead they were driving over rolling hills heavily furred with golden wheat. "Where are we going?" he asked.

"I thought we'd visit a coffee shop in Garfield," she said. "That way Rafe can't drop in on us. I want to get this straight,

Tom. I want to know about mental junk. I think I've let things slide too far."

Tom crossed his arms over his stomach, clutching his elbows. She had raised Rafe. Look who *he* was. How could Tom trust her? What could he do if she betrayed him? Move on—maybe back to Aunt Herbacea—and start all over again.

Tingle.

He slumped down to unbend his pocket, then reached in and found the heart. —Wait, he thought, pulling his hand out with the heart in it. He glanced at his aunt. She smiled at him before her face settled back into sad. He decided she would accept his silence. Garfield was still fifteen minutes away. He leaned back and closed his eyes again.

—Hannah?

Webs of sensation spun up his arm, little spiders walking up his insides to touch his mind.

—Hannah, who are you? What are you?

—I'm lost. Now you found me. I don't know what happened, I was really sick, but I couldn't tell Mama, she never wants to know. You ever have days when you try to touch things but they all seem to be behind glass? And it kept getting thicker, it got between me and my own self. I remember pulling on Mama's apron, saying Mama Mama Mama but it was like I wasn't there. She was talking to someone and she walked across the room fast and through the door and I ran into the wall, I wasn't watching. I don't think she ever saw me again. Then another time it was night and I went to the park and laid down and thought about it and nobody looked for me. I couldn't feel my fingers. I couldn't feel my toes. I couldn't feel my knees or my face or my elbows after a while, not warm nor cold nor rain when it started, nor grass nor mosquitoes nor anything. In the morning somebody found me and took me away but I stayed there, Tommy. Nothing to touch. Nothing to feel or hear or see or taste or do or do or do. Now it's different. I like the way you look at things.

The tingles began to spread down his chest, streaking across him like a rain of sparkler fire. He tensed up. He opened his eyes and his palm. The golden heart was shrinking into his fate, heart, head and life lines.

"Hannah!" he said aloud.

His aunt swerved the car, then got back into her own lane. "What? Tom! Don't do that!"

—I won't hurt you, Hannah thought. Tingles cascaded down his back, down his other arm, through his groin, down his legs. —I can help you. I'll notice things for you. You get those self-under-glass days. I know you do. I'll help you keep in touch.

"Hannah," he moaned. Tingles reached his toes. The last gleam of gold in his palm vanished.

His aunt drove over onto the shoulder of the road and stopped the car. "Tom, what happened? Are you all right, sweetie?"

He looked at his aunt's face made new. Friendly iced-tea-colored eyes with crow's-foot corners, a worry dent like an up-side-down T above her round-ended nose; full lips an unlikely shade of orange; the whole firm roundness of her face framed in silver-streaked balsa-brown curls. He reached up, watched his hand tremble, watched it touch her cheek. His fingertips sizzled with sensations of softness, peach fuzz, powder, firm flesh under velvet. Real life. Not next door. Not glimpsed and forgotten. Inside him. The smell of sun-warmed seat covers, stale cigarettes, his aunt's antiperspirant and his own self, still slightly sweaty from his earlier run, and the sun-broiled asphalt and sun-ripened wheat outside. The ticking of the engine, the faint whispering tides of their breath moving in and out of them, the louder whispers of wheat stalks sliding against each other in the nearly still afternoon air.

"Tommy!"

Her voice seemed a blending of so many tones, all somehow harmonized. He looked at her, waiting for more.

"Tom. Answer me this instant or I'll scream."

"Aunt. Rose. Oh, nuts." He rubbed his eyes and tried to wake into a reacting state. —Hannah, don't hypnotize me.

—It's *soooo* beautiful.

He put his hands over his eyes. —I don't know if I can take this!

—I'm not leaving. I won't hurt you, but I'm not leaving.

"Talk to me, Tommy. Who's Hannah? What happened?"

"It doesn't make any sense, Aunt Rose."

"What doesn't make sense?"

—Can I trust her?

—Yes, thought Hannah. —If it doesn't work, you still have me.

How peculiar. Never to be alone again? "I found this thing in the grass this morning," he began, and told her everything. He even told her about thinking of giving the heart to Rafe. "He keeps telling me that if I don't do what he wants, he'll convince you I'm crazy and you'll send me away." He looked down at his hands. "I don't want to go away, Au— Rose. Especially now. I have this new friend inside me. Maybe I am crazy."

"Maybe you are," she said. She stared out at the wheat. "You picked up a gold thing and it melted into you. It's the soul of a girl. You have a girl inside you? Can she speak for herself?"

"No!" Tom said. "I don't want her to talk. She might get too real."

He and his aunt looked at each other. Rosemary's forehead wrinkled. She bit her lower lip.

"I have to think about this. Let's go home," she said. She lit a cigarette, started the engine, turned the car around and headed back to town.

After she parked in the driveway, he climbed out and stretched, enjoying the tightening and loosening of every muscle. He yawned and turned to smile at his aunt. No answering smile. He sobered.

Rafe waited for them in the front hall. "Mom?"

"What, dear?"

"You didn't go shopping."

"No, we didn't." She turned on the hall light and looked at him.

"Are you all right?"

Tom admired him for the nineteenth time. He sounded so solicitous, Tom felt like having himself committed.

"No, Rafe, I'm not all right. I feel like any mother would if she discovered her son was a blackmailer. I love you, Rafe. You are my only child, and I loved your father very much. I understand jealousy too. But I don't like this sick way you respond to it. Talk to me. Tell me how you feel about having your cousin live with us. Don't waste all your energy making him miserable. This is not a good way for a human being to live."

"What did he say about me? He lies a lot, Mom. We don't really know him."

"I don't know him very well, but his father was your father's twin brother, same face, same genes, same character. The same warmth. Tommy is like his father."

"But Mom—but Mom . . ." Rafe's face crumpled, lost maturity. "You don't know. He's not safe. He has a dark side he can't control—"

Tom felt himself fading, fading, thinning. A boy-shaped volume of mist about to dissipate. —Oh, no you don't, thought Hannah. —I did that once. Never again. Nobody will come looking for us if we disappear. We have to find each other. We have to make ourselves real, and reach through the glass, to touch life. Talk, stupid.

"Rose, you asked me questions," said Tom. "I didn't volunteer. You must have believed Rafe was doing something to me. You know Rafe." Tom clutched his elbows, felt muscles tighten across the tops of his shoulders. "I'll go upstairs and pack. But I want my pictures and my ring back before I leave, Rafe." —Smash my present, but leave me my past. Hannah, I'm going to need you.

—I'm here.

Rosemary looked from one to the other. Tom wondered if she was deciding whether to commit him. "Rafe. Give me this much. Don't force me to choose between you. If I send him away, I'll hate you and myself for it. If he stays and you keep sabotaging him, I'll go crazy. Tell me the truth, Rafe. Make the snarl straighten out."

The silence stretched. At last Rafe said, "I guess he can stay," in a hard bright voice. He smiled at Tom, one of the old mean smiles.

Tom opened his mouth. "Thank you," said Hannah's little-girl voice. Tom watched as Rafe's smile dissolved into fear.

Not for the world would I spoil your pleasure in this elegant little story by giving you even a hint about it.

FLAWLESS EXECUTION

BY DEAN WESLEY SMITH

The man stood poised on the stone ledge of the twelfth-floor balcony, arms forward, feet together in the classic stance of the professional diver. He wore red trunks. He was suntanned and well muscled. He slowly lowered his arms to his sides, staring out over the buildings of the city.

The crowd in the streets below hushed.

He signaled to the judges with a nod that he was ready. Cameras started.

He took a step forward and then sprang upward.

The dive was perfect. His brown body floated past the upper judges with ever-increasing speed.

One and a half.

Two and a half . . . pike . . . then out.

Twist.

Three and a half . . . another twist.

Four and a half . . . another twist.

Back into pike. Then into layout again. Then one final, extremely slow layout and his body hit the sidewalk flat, face down.

Perfect.

The crowd cheered wildly, then quieted in anticipation.

$9\frac{1}{2}$ . . . $9\frac{1}{2}$ . . . 9 . . . $8\frac{1}{2}$ . . . $8\frac{1}{2}$ . . . $9\frac{1}{2}$ . . . 9 . . . 9 . . . $9\frac{1}{2}$

The nine judges flashed their verdict in eight-foot-tall electronic numbers in a row up the side of the building beside their stations.

The crowd yelled, clapped, stamped their feet in enthusiastic agreement. The television networks ran slow-motion playbacks with expert commentary.

Another diver took his place on the ledge.

The crowd calmed to low talking and whispers. They knew he was the favorite. He had killed his wife and children. His attorney had kept him on death row through a series of appeals for an extra month, simply so he could practice more.

The diver raised his arms in front of him and stood poised. Below him, the clean-up crew finished hosing down the sidewalk and stepped back.

The crowd held its breath and waited.

There are some stories that you don't want to explain: you just want to say, "Here, for God's sake, read this."

GEOMETRY

BY JAN HERSCHEL

He was looking at the slanted patch of sunlight coming through the doorway. The sun was shining from the north, still high above the veranda; that meant the crates of milk would still be in the shade under the peppercorn tree.

He turned and looked through the window to the traffic-lights where the cars pulled up and waited and then drove off with a long slash of sunlight along the chrome and then the blank asphalt grey until the next car followed with the next perfect slash. If all the cars had been the same with the same line of chrome the pattern need never have been broken, he thought. You'd never have to watch the dark grey road stretched over the ground like solid grey dirt with petrol-pumps suddenly stuck in it. The asphalt just ran out at the edges as though it had been spilt; there wasn't a step at the edge between the asphalt and the petrol station. The asphalt was formless.

He began to draw the chrome car in his mind; he rearranged the traffic so that the pattern would continue in a rhythm all day every day, so that it would blink in rhythmical dazzles that would continue out past the sun forever, be a line forever through space.

It was geometry. The teacher was drawing on the board and explaining and telling them not to talk. They had to draw a thirty-degree angle, a forty-five-degree angle, and a sixty-degree angle. The nut in his compass was loose and he couldn't tighten it and the pencil always slipped.

He looked at the crack in the wall over his left shoulder. It ran in zigzags like little gapings, as though it was a solid line of ants, and then petered out below the pot-plants. He wedged himself against the wall and put his ruler and pencil-sharpener behind the pencil-groove on his desk.

He was always fascinated by the straight creases down the arms of his shirt when it was ironed. By putting your arm straight out you could draw a line from yourself to anything; if you squinted the line didn't even bump at your fist.

His pencil had slipped. He reached into his bag for his rubber. It wasn't there. He remembered he'd forgotten it on his desk at home and if he'd gone back for it he would've missed the bus and been late. He looked along the pencil-grooves on the rows of desks. Michael didn't have one. Arnoldo had one but he was on the other side of the room. And Arnoldo wouldn't lend him one anyway.

The teacher was still marking the homework at her desk. He turned around. Anthony was sitting behind him, his tongue stuck out like a blob among the small blotches of his freckles. There was a brown rubber on Anthony's desk, dark and clammy where Anthony had sweated on it.

He watched Anthony's hand moving, Anthony writing with a pencil-stub that fitted into the cave between his palm and the page, making small noises as though he was counting. Suddenly he remembered them all learning to count, and the jagged line of Anthony's warm wet piss staining the floor and creeping towards him.

He looked back at the printed blue lines on the creamy white page, the fine grey pencil-lines intersecting them and lurching crazily into nowhere when the pressure on the compass had changed.

"Anthony," he whispered. Everyone else kept working, so the teacher couldn't've heard. Anthony hadn't heard either. His head was still bent and his left hand was like a dirty paw around his diagram, making a grey fog of pencil-smudge where the lines joined. He bent his first finger and poked Anthony's arm with his knuckle, but not hard enough so that it would hurt too much for him to say yes.

"Anthony, rubber?" Anthony looked up with the ends of his hair poking into his eyes and his mouth open. He nodded. "Give it back," he whispered. His nose was blocked.

He took the rubber and cleaned it and rubbed out the jagged arc. Anthony would lend anyone anything, he thought, because whatever he had was always small and dirty and worthless. He drew the arc again. The pencil slipped again. He rubbed half the arc out again and put the rubber in the pencil-groove on his desk. It was an ink-rubber; it was rubbing the blue lines out as well as the pencil ones. He could draw the blue lines back in afterwards. And if Anthony wanted the rubber back he could ask for it. Anthony's diagram would be a black-grey smudgy mess whether he had a rubber or not.

He wondered if the men in the cars at the intersection needed geometry. He supposed they must've learnt it, but he couldn't imagine anything like geometry in their jobs. They couldn't've drawn lines and arcs, the way their suits were crumpled. His father was an accountant. That was arithmetic.

A ruler poked him in the back. "Rubber," Anthony whispered. Loud and hurt and stupid.

"Anthony! Come out the front!"

Everyone looked up. The teacher's face had been red and pinched all the morning. Anyone could've seen she'd be furious.

Anthony went out the front and stood facing the blackboard with his head hanging down. Anthony's head *would* be hanging down, he thought. The teacher crossed the raised part of the floor to the cupboard to get the strap.

"I thought I told all of you not to talk! And as for you. It's not as though your work is anything to talk about. And whoever talked to this boy first should be out here as well."

The strap was hitting Anthony's hand, a thick, vicious, hitting-on-flesh sound. Nobody looked at him as he came down the aisle between the desks. He watched Anthony sit down and put his head in his arms. He was crying.

He poked him on the arm with the rubber, trying to give it back. Anthony didn't look up.

"I'll get you a new one."

Anthony still wasn't looking up. His head was still buried; his hair pricked unevenly over the sleeves of his jumper. It had holes in the arms where the check shirt showed through. The school uniform was supposed to be a blue shirt. He pricked him on the hand with his compass-point. A small point of blood oozed up.

"Anthony! I said I'll get you a new one!"

Anthony looked up. His face was red and blotched and bleary as though piss was oozing through it.

"Go away," he said, and rubbed the back of his hand over his face. He buried his head again, smearing the point of blood down from his eye.

At recess-time he got a bottle of milk from the milk-crates. Anthony wasn't there. He must be in the toilets. He took the cap off the milk and went to find him. Anthony was crouched against the corner on the cement in a wet patch that never dried. His arms were around his shoulders and head. He put the milk down beside him, just past the wet mark.

"Here," he said. Anthony didn't say anything. He looked at the bottom of the milk-bottle. It was wet with condensation running down the sides. Making a new puddle. Anthony sniffed.

He got up and walked towards the door. He heard Anthony get up. He turned and a gobbeted arc of milk sprayed over him. "It's your fault!" Anthony was choking, and ran past him like an animal out through the doorway while he stood there, the milk dribbling over his shorts and down his legs.

He wiped off as much as he could. He took his shirt off and stuck it under the tap.

Anthony's place was empty; he'd run away home. Nobody talked. The rubber stayed on Anthony's desk.

His shirt stuck to his back and arms. He looked out the window. The cars were flickering past less often because it was late and most of the men had gone to work. The asphalt stretched out from the frayed and meandering edges of the footpaths like a grey sea that had no reason to stop at its own edges, as though when it turned liquid and shimmered in the heat nothing would stop it spreading everywhere, running over the footpaths and into the floors. When he looked down he could see the outlines of the milk-stains through the drying water on his clothes.

Anthony's mother brought him back at lunch-time; he saw her talking to the teacher. Anthony was over by the bike-racks, by himself, kicking the dirt and stones near the shadow of the shed where they had lunch.

When he went up to him Anthony looked at him and turned away and went scuffling into the shadows. His shoes sounded as though they weren't done up; the scuffle-sounds were hollow. When he followed him into the shade his shirt kept moving coldly against his ribs.

"Hey, Anthony," he said, and Anthony hunched his shoulder and suddenly he was grabbing him, hitting him and pulling him onto the ground. Anthony was crying even though it couldn't've hurt much and in there in the shadows he thought I'll give you something to cry about while the cars flickered dry and shining past the cyclone fence along the dry asphalt along the dry painted traffic-lines.

He picked up a stone and while Anthony's chest and throat and shoulders and legs and arms were squirming under him he dragged the stone down Anthony's calf.

The cut was bleeding. He stood up and Anthony ran off crying.

Anthony's mother and the teacher were looking at him over the desert of dirt and yellow stones. The teacher was coming towards him. He was going to be caned in front of the others. Who wouldn't look at him. Except Anthony, who would look up at him with his hair in his eyes, and watch him and hate him while the cut on his leg turned into a scar, and the scab broke off in sections like the chrome strips dazzling in the rhythmical, never-ending line.

Here is a lapidary story about a woman's devotion to the beautiful animals she has bred and trained, and to their ancient way of life.

ONE LAST HUNTING PACK

BY PATRICIA LINEHAN

Orlayin craned her neck to watch the bright-red patrol flyer zig-zag quietly, methodically, up the gully until it disappeared into a diminishing bank of cumulus. So, the famous Canadian Reds were hunting too, even this far from their border. Her hand reached to stroke Jada's muzzle, to stay the insistent poking into her armpit. With trembling fingers she traced the prominent veins of the Borzoi's long chiseled face, gently tapping the cold nose which protruded into the air like a great Roman cliff. A wet tongue cleaned her thumb. The smell of dog was warm, this close, their bodies pressed together under the protection of a low-spreading juniper. Jada always dove in next to her; she never got enough attention. She was, perhaps, the cleverest, but all the dogs had learned quickly. *Flyer. I fall. You fall. Stay hidden.*

The rest of the pack lay scattered under the bushes, almond-shaped black eyes fastened on Orlayin, tongues dripping hot droplets of saliva onto dry ponderosa needles. They watched silently, frozen, slender necks arched into the low tree branches.

Orlayin sat up stiffly, brushing leaf fragments from her chest. The dogs stood and shook off the twigs and debris that clung to their fine coats. "You were very good. Good dogs. All of you were good dogs."

Jada. Yon. Jamis. Kindra. Kira. Scotia. They crowded around her, the game done, pushing past each other, bowling the Loved over with their narrow heads and thin hound legs. Paws scraped at the sleeves of her torn jacket.

"Stop," she laughed. Then, "Stop," without laughter. Command.

Jamis raised his grizzled lips to Kindra, who was not stopping, was not leaving room for the Leader. Kindra lowered her scarred muzzle to the ground and peed, baring her pink belly to his fangs. She was very young.

"Knock it off." Orlayin thumped Jamis on the head. He wasn't a very tolerant grandfather, but damn, he could still course. "We'll go hungry tonight unless we work fast." She talked over their heads, looking down the gully to where it spread out into a smudge of brown mountain clearing. The smell of the pine trees seeped into her pores. It would be a beautiful place to settle, the San Juans, but what fantasy. Now there was only forward, or sideways, or backtrack. Evasion until they could reach the southern border and slip into Mexico and safety.

A pond reflected the late afternoon sun from the base of the steep ridge. With the dusk, whitetails would be coming down to water soon, and though the clearing was small, if they deployed they should be able to make a kill. The dogs understood deployment innately. "Come along."

The seven picked a careful way down the slopes, between scrub pine and lichened boulders. Despite the exercise, Orlayin shivered, the cold stabbing her left knee again. To keep her mind off the arthritis she puffed her breath out in huffing clouds to amuse the dogs. Their faces steamed like engines. Their toes gripped the talus like cats' paws.

Orlayin fell behind them to admire. Her weathered face crinkled into a proud brown grin. Scotia's limp was gone. Good. He would need his soundness. Jamis was so evident in all of them. Heavy bone. And the old Kelcrest bitch too was there. She had had that prepotent wide truck rear, the stifle bent low and wide, the second thigh long and strong. Finally had that rear set too, it came through every generation. Or had for five. Oh, there were a few minor alterations to make here and there yet. Finer ear leather, blacker pigment . . . the connoisseur's crotchets. Another three generations would have finished the sculpture. They would have been the highest kind of beauty—form and function flowing together. Orlayin sucked the dog smell and forest smell deeply into her lungs. It was a sculpture that deserved to be finished, but you didn't raise litters running from the law.

She touched Jamis gently on the head, her thick fingers stroking his silvered skull. The dogs were filled out with hard muscle. Even under a coming winter coat, Kira's shoulders rippled with each sloping stride. Her shoulders were a bit loaded, Orlayin decided, but she'd never passed that on. Besides, she had a topline like Tatiana's bronze.

A raven screamed overhead, circling in the spotty clouds. The dogs stopped and stared, their eyes watching the spreading of the wing tips, the fanning of the tail; their thin ears unfolded forward in six matador caps of concern. Orlayin smiled at them. Their curves fitted into the woods like wind, a bending thing. Beauty and Bringers of Death. They all took the responsibility of death where no one else would . . . where the law made sure no one would. Dry twigs crackled under their weight as the pack started up again.

Fire would be nice. Warmth. Orlayin blew on the stubby knotted knuckles of her stiff hands. No gloves. Should have foreseen the Unity would get serious and raid even the remote areas; should have been prepared. She pressed her palms against the warmth of her cheeks. If they could just make it past Marble Canyon by November there was still some bleak hope. But even if it snowed before then they still had to stick to the mountains. On the plains they'd be killed without a chance. No cover . . . besides, the people would turn them in. They had their entertainment machines, their fat bellies; no struggles, no chaos, no choices, and boredom. The towns were all peopled by tamed and yapping pets.

At least Mexico had laughed at the world from their oil-sodden ground. A man still looked at blood on his hands there. Getting over the border had been difficult enough before, but now with the Canadian Reds in the hunt? She shook her head. What did it matter to them that somewhere there was life going on? Threatening. Too threatening. And it was the duty of the police of all nations in the Unity to take away all threats, all dangers, all struggles; and leave blobs.

Of course the Canadians would be more than tickled to take a share of the dogs. They were probably just in it for that. Real coursing Borzoi were quite a prize. Maybe these were even the last in the world. No. No, surely in the Soviet Union someone had saved them. Some artist, some poet, some peasant must have managed to slip from the city and run with her hounds. What was she like, that one? Orlayin touched Kira's flank lightly. What was that woman like? When she held each squirming whelp under, did her tears distress the water into vanishing circles? Did the zoo or the museums terrify her more?

Here, if they were caught, the Unity Police Institute in D.C. would get most of them. But the Canadians, for their help now, would take two or three dogs on up to Montreal's grandest Museum of Natural History, or Criminal History. Whichever was biggest. Maybe they'd get Jada; poise her in flight, forever tucked in a tight diving run. They'd probably have her chasing a bunny, for Christ's sake, and they wouldn't know how to snake the tail like a rudder for an inside turn. Poor Jada.

Orlayin looked at her hounds. To see them coursing, to see them bringing down game, was to watch ghosts of ghosts, racing for breath. They flowed leanly between the trees like Druids. Oh, God. Futile. She blinked back the tears that wanted to slip into the deep creases around her eyes. Quickly. Before the dogs could see. One embraced one's decisions. The dogs didn't know about the law anyway, so they couldn't agonize over the stupidity of its enforcement; over the stupidity of pellet eaters fleeing the wholeness of beast against beast.

An hour before dusk the pack reached the upper edge of the clearing. A breeze flowed over the pond and into their nostrils, but the Borzoi only casually tested for scents, never trusting their poor noses. Gazehounds, they waited to see.

Scotia, Jamis and Yon carefully scouted down the rim of the forest. Orlayin squinted after them as long as the red and silver and white of their coats could be glimpsed through the underbrush. She would wait with the bitches for the males to flush game. Jada tensed under her stroking hand and sniffed the air, quivering. Kira gathered her powerful haunches beneath her loins in readiness. Kindra stood and stared, ears out, tail in a slow low wag.

Orlayin watched the clearing. A whitetail doe suddenly rose out of the tall grass beside the pond. Scotia burst from the woods, a silver flying phantasm. Jamis overtook him in six bounds, his pasterns bending flat against the earth, back flexing with each straining leap like a bullwhip. Yon flew wide to the opposite side to trap the doe and drive her into waiting jaws. Lean heads sliced into the wind, slim bladed bones cutting through the air, their eyes glistening with effort and joy.

The whitetail stood, unblinking. A mallard cried and beat his wings against the dark water, flapping wildly across the pond and up into the chill. Still unmoving, the doe stared serenely. The dogs raced, heads low, coiling, uncoiling.

"No! Run! Run!" Orlayin screamed. "Run!" She stumbled into the clearing, waving her arms at the males. She felt her gray matted hair flap like an anguished halo about her screeching face. The deer wasn't moving! "Go back! No! Go back! It isn't real! Go back! Back!"

Jamis stopped, his sons panting behind him. Puzzled and worried, they obeyed and paced through the reeds at the far edge of the pond, sides heaving, tongues hanging past their long chipped teeth.

Kindra's turn. She bounded toward the deer, eyes sparkling, fangs bared, her growl song far down in her throat. She stretched into the air, the deep chest expanding, knobbed pasterns pumping the breeze, fine golden fur billowing about her neck.

"No! No, Kindra!"

The puppy hesitated, then swung to circle behind her prey.

"Don't touch it!" Orlayin dove for her. Electricity crackled in a pure blue arc from the metal grid beneath the grass, joining Kindra in midstride, dancing with her in jerking rhythms down to the dried wild flowers.

The rest of the Borzoi ran.

"Shit. I sure thought they'd catch the lot. If you ask me, they're getting sloppy." The Canadian apprentice hopped slowly from one large foot to the other, grinding stiff tufts of hair into the floor. "It's damned cold down here."

"You get used to it. Crank the spreader up three notches. I have to seal the interior again."

The apprentice widened the gap between the dog's new plastic ribs so that the Master Taxidermist could spray a fourth coat of sealant over every tanned interior pore. "That stuff stinks."

"Yes, but it's effective. Take her down now and lay her over there." He pointed to an oak table against the frosted cement wall and turned to pull a bag of brown spheres out of his desk drawer.

She couldn't weigh over twenty pounds, the apprentice thought. He stood on a stool and lifted Kindra in his arms but she didn't come loose. The goddamned hooks always gave him trouble. He struggled with the heavy steel suspensor that dug into the dog's empty abdominal cavity and out her anus.

"Trouble?" The Master was waiting patiently by the table.

"I always have trouble with these damned things."

"Here. Let me show you." With slender manicured hands, the Taxidermist angled the form and lifted it up and off. "It's in the tilt." He carried the dog over to the wall.

"Sure would have been something to get them all, don't you think? This isn't going to make much of a display. And here the Committee cleaned out the entrance case for a major attraction." The apprentice returned to a steady hopping, pulling his jacket sleeves down over his cold hands.

The Master patted Kindra's head. "It will still be splendid, absolutely splendid." He picked up a scalpel. "Getting the eyes right is hard, so you pay attention now. If you learn to get the eyes right, you'll be famous." Kindra's muzzle rested stiffly in his left hand. His fingers traced the delicate veining of her profile. "I have more work in the Hall than all the Journeymen put together. Why? Because I can do eyes like no one else. Forms?

Child's play. The eyes make the display." He brushed the puppy's fine gold lashes with one edge of the scalpel.

"Take her eyes, for instance. They'll have to be keen, so they look through you like they're staring hard into the past. They call that the look of eagles. But they'll have to be soft too; and it's damned hard to get keen and soft in the same expression. I hope I can do it again. I haven't had a sighthound since the Scottish pack was flushed in MacDurmy." The Master Taxidermist chuckled and bent over the head. "You think they're getting sloppy here? It took the Island Unity Police two whole years to catch that McVorney and his deerhounds. What a display that made in London. I did it, you know. Have I told you about that?"

"A hundred times," the apprentice laughed. He played with Kindra's tail, flopping it back and forth on the tabletop, warming his hands in the dense fur. "Who'd have thought that old woman could've survived and crawled away? Sloppy, I'm telling you. Real sloppy."

"The trappers can't be everywhere at once. It wasn't their fault. The grid short-circuited next to the pond water, that's all. The voltage wasn't up enough. They'll catch her." The Master slipped a light brown sphere into the puppy's empty eye socket and began to paint in the look of eagles.

"Well, when they do get her, how're you going to do her eyes?"

"Just like I did McVorney's. Criminal, of course. That's what they all are. Pure criminal."

Who was the innovator who first wrote of a human-alien contact from the alien's viewpoint? Not Wells, not Fitz-James O'Brien. Even Stanley G. Weinbaum, whose work in its antic humor this story somewhat resembles, followed the Victorian dictum that the strange must always be framed by the familiar; and Weinbaum wrote in the early thirties. Somewhere in the crumbling pulp magazines of the forties, I suspect, is a forgotten story, the first to break this barrier; but I will leave that discovery to others.

Meanwhile, here is as delightful an example of the alien-viewpoint story as I have ever seen. You are about to enter the twilit world of the Slinkies and follow them in their epic battles from Languishing Rock to the Desert Crystallith, and from the Feeding Quakemass to the Lesser Emberdusk . . .

THE COMING OF THE GOONGA

GARY W. SHOCKLEY

It is the Crepuscular Greatdawn, time when the twin suns track together above the Spire Mounts and the double shadows grow long. In the Orange Basin near Calep there are close-knit shadows of precise geometry not to be found elsewhere. We hide beyond their stretch and contemplate their source, the spot where a shortseason ago the pods fell, and where in a few days the industrious aliens fashioned their fabulous base. On murknights when the echo-cloud blots out the twin suns, we can see three dashing stars. These we know to be their mother ships.

They are truly great builders, they who call themselves "human."

Our zeromaster Batinka predicts a good year. This is disconcerting to us, for it is the remarkable talent of a zeromaster always to be wrong. Early in her long reign Batinka scribed long lists of animal viscera; later, suffering chokeblossom fever, she spent days scribing, "Spare the Treader of the Painted Leaf"; later still she scribed a line so perfectly straight that we could see no deviation for a hundredflop. These and other prophecies, if such they be, defeat our understanding. These we ballast with the years and let sink to haunt our inner minds. But Batinka is topical and clear when she mentions "visitors from the mountain of the sky." Many close friendships will develop between our kinds, she says, and all will profit from our cooperative ventures. This is a prophecy indeed for the outer mind, and it fills us with trepidation.

Among the frozen and sharp-edged shadows there is one that is neither, which distorts wildly across the others till its tip nearly touches our concealment. The one they call Lola walks near the outskirts of the base. She stops when she comes upon the one they call Roxanne. Faintly we hear the mingling of their voices.

We have our own names for these two. Lola we call Awakener because our Watchers wake us when she appears (we have instructed them to do so). She knows no schedule, is apt to rise at any hour to go prowling through the night. This she did a few hours ago and walked eastward through the jezelles to the edge of our ancestral slicks. We are ever fascinated by the way she touches things, peers at them close up with her device, and remarks upon them to her wrist. Sometimes she collects the things she studies, putting them in collapsible bubbles. But she is ever careful not to disturb what she suspects is ours. The humans know of our presence and our intelligence, but Awakener alone respects us. She has given us a name: slinkies. It is a better one than yeddeenians, which we call ourselves. I use it always now.

Her function remains unclear. She speaks often with the cooks, pointing to the things she has collected, but at greater length she speaks to those crouched in constant vigil over complex implements. We think that she is a foodsmith, though her small skin pores suggest a weathersnapper.

The other, the one they call Roxanne, we call Loud Giant. She is taller by a head than Awakener and certainly much taller than we, and her voice carries above the moontoad's. But the basis for her name goes further, to the nature of her exploits. For she will start a war with our kind. Noisy, devastating, it will bring death to four of every five slinkies. This I know because those times have come and gone, this being written after the fact. I use the present tense to describe the past, because I must. It is my curse, but also my blessing, for it sustains me. The present is my salvation.

Our Watchers sometimes venture into the base in the cloaked hours to peer through the transparent membranes. Some have even entered the structures. They tell us knowingly of the soft-soil mound where Loud Giant and Awakener lie together, unsheathed, like fevered jungle mudsquabs. This memory arouses my jealousy and calls to mind Loud Giant's own at the time: while she gives all her love to Awakener, Awakener gives hers to many—to Janice, Sarah, Roger, Bill. . . . Loud Giant once made Bill's face bleed and threatened the others. But it gained her nothing; Awakener would not speak to her for a stark moon. Now they are friends once more and have spent this morning together.

We, the slinkies, can understand Loud Giant's jealousy. We are monogamists with few exceptions. We take one mate for life, another for death. This does not mean we despise Awakener for her ways. Indeed, she is loved by all, watched by all, as much the favorite of our kind as of theirs.

Awakener, as I am saying, pauses to speak with Loud Giant. We, working some distance away under cover of huehair and weewoochuntz, admire the agility of her many-jointed body (today her carapace is seafoam blue with flecks of silver) and sense joy in her every gesture. Though she is not slinkie, there is a richness of expression about her that strikes us as very beauti—

"Op!" the conjuremaster Pedeet barks my name. I shake free of entrancement and see that inattention has let the goonga grow restless. (Awakener calls our goongas "bagpipes," but I prefer our name.) It is trying to belly out. That would kink its eight long snouts or dislodge the slender hollow reeds we have fitted in their ends. Jentzoot and Kamin prod it from this urge while I apply myself to fondling. Soon it quivers with only one wish. I communicate this fact to the pointers, who load; then I slip about to the glands. I am pleasantly surprised to have a clear view of Loud Giant and Awakener as I fondle and squeeze.

The seconds become vivid. Awakener is laughing, has finished a gesture, must talk louder than she would like because of the hums and rattles of nearby machinery. Beyond the shadows where we of the goonga patrol lurk, these sounds are nearly lost. We hear instead the stridencies of the winged lamoor, the bray of the dozerwomp, the chatter-clack of rocksips . . . and the coming of the goonga.

The latter is a sharp "whoof," almost a thunderclap, and the goonga's fierce compaction sends me sprawling. But not for an instant do I lose sight of the pair.

Awakener is not at first responsive to the faint jarring that afflicts her. She talks a moment longer before seeing the alarm registering upon Loud Giant's face. Only then does she look down upon her own body and see the eight fibrillances piercing her chest and stomach, pinning her against the structure behind. She squints, perhaps seeing the tiny wellings of blood at the entry points. Her eyes go wide, her mouth is open and silently working. It is then that she moves and in this way chooses her moment to expire. . . .

It is the Painting Season, the time to suggest to nature a new attire. As in past seasons I choose the zigzag leaf. Always have I felt that it lacks something in shape and venation. After all, the zigzag trees that shadow the Evernight deserve the finest of calling cards. For two weeks I labor over it, dyeing it, trimming its irregular outline, adding ribs and veins and the faintest hint of spots. I take it to the nature festival where everyone shows their renderings of leaf, bark, stone, grass, moss, and even skyscape. Afterward we return our suggestions to the field for nature to consider. And next year we will see how she has judged them.

Loud Giant catches Awakener as she twists and sags with seafoam carapace bursting red. Their shadows sharply retreat as one escorts the other to the ground, to a sleep from which Awakener will never awaken; and there, rocking her in her arms, Loud Giant suddenly looks up with trouncelot eyes. She looks out, toward our position. And she bellows. She bellows and is running at us. Awakener extinguishes her own shadow in a final sprawl that turns the bottom of her left boot toward us. There we can see my painted leaf.

Long ago Batinka wrote, "Spare the Treader of the Painted Leaf," and we did not know its meaning. Now we do, and, though buried by a score of years, that behest must now be honored, must now be disobeyed. We are sorry, Awakener. We are truly sorry.

I try to coax the goonga back to its underground safe haven. The conjuremaster, the pointers, and the prodders have fled, lacking my compassion, or perhaps I their wits. Suddenly Loud Giant stands over me, a rock uplifted beside her red-tasseled head. The moment is uncertain; she emotes fiercely: "I will kill every last one of you! Do you understand? Every last one! Tell the rest. Tell them they will all die by my hand. Tell them!" She hurls the rock far over my head, turns and retraces her steps.

How can one not be impressed by the suddenness, the singleness, the utterness of her decision? Among my kind, to commit oneself even briefly to a course of action is rare, and regardless of its overall merit it deserves the highest praise—for it suggests zeromaster blood. It is, I think, at this moment, as I sit watching the guttering retreat of Loud Giant's fierce long shadow, that I begin to love her.

We will meet again, many times, over the course of the war, which will span three years and see our kind's steady retreat across the Great Sinking Ocherlands, through the Desert Crystallith, over the Shaglands of Ordorn, and back again. Near the midpoint of the war we will meet near the Shaddocks of Trite and there I will be killed. And a year later, at war's end, a similar fate will find her. Of such things are great tragedies written. Yet this is not as it seems; this will not be tragedy. Nor do I scribe the horrors of war, of which there were certainly many. Nor a grand heroic epic to please the minions. My perspective is different. I perceive and live the war as an elaborate courtship, elegant in its rituals, uncompromising in its expressions of love. As such will I describe it. Only when it serves my purpose will I delve into the finer aspects of war. Let me now begin to tell the things that were and have become.

There is confusion and dismay among our droves as the humans, led by Loud Giant and others, venture into our territories and begin the slaughter. We wait for our zeromaster to instruct us. In ten days our number in the Enumerated Lands is halved, and we fear for the survival of our species. It is then that our zeromaster's words reach us: "Surrender to an enemy whose weapons speak louder than yours; do not prolong the inevitable defeat; do not expend lives in a lost cause." With these words we are committed to winning the war.

There are fifty-seven in the drove to which I humbly belong. The first major skirmish is ours, at Hasson Cove near the Windgate. I, a fondler among many, lead us to slaughter with my staggering incompetence. I bring my goonga to discharge too quickly, so that it spends the fibrillances at the enemy's feet, serving to warn rather than to harm. Near me is Geesha, the one that I then love. She works her goonga expertly and still works it as I flee. She does not survive the skirmish. Later, upon the Feeding Quakemoss east of the Quenchant, my conjuremaster disciplines me for my impatience. I accept the splinters without protest, though I know my behavior was soundly inspired. Loud Giant was leading her troops. I feared she would fall in the first volley. That must not happen. Not yet—not till we are closer to the Evernight.

It is six skirmishes later that our retreat brings us through the low Ocherlands, where it is convenient for us to pay the Manuscriptors of Evernight a formal visit. Most are in the mating coves, and their passionate grappling/signaling for an instant strikes me as countless pairs of human hands swinging boom-weapons about to fire, to pierce us with lances we can never find —invisilances, we call them. But my imagination wanders far afield. We pass by the mating coves and come to the nutrient glades. There we see what the Manuscriptors have scrawled that day.

Some who read this may be human. For those I should digress. We, the slinkies, do not bury our dead. Once we shared that ritual with you, but no more. We take our dead to the outer glades and feed each to a single healthy full-grown squab who has failed to run the Labyrinth. A squab that runs the Labyrinth has already consumed a higher intelligence, and it is not good to join it with a second. The squab remains a squab; its basic needs remain its basic needs. But should one supply it with all that it requires, placing it upon a glade of nutrient, its primitive intelligence relaxes enough to let the other flicker through. The only physical manifestation the slinkie mind can effect is control over the crawlpath. It is in this way—through the written word—that our dead communicate with us. The present tense must prevail, for the squab is a creature of the present moment, and to use the past tense is to disturb its sense of well-being, which leads to suppression.

The first message reaching us from one new to the Evernight will be an afterwish. If it is deemed reasonable, and possible, those closest to the deceased must grant it. Should we of the first life want to communicate something to a Manuscriptor, we write upon the nutrient with a concentrate of the same and place the squab at the proper end. The slinkie mind and the squab itself have poor eyesight, but while the squab inexorably follows the concentrate, the slinkie mind can read words from its motion.

Today we hope to learn from those who perished in recent battles. Standing beneath a zigzag tree that contributes a generous swath of shade to the Evernight, I peer out upon the chaotic lines of those who died in terror and did not recover. Less salient are the long tedious epic poems indulged in by so many dead warriors. Still others are tiny neat scribbles, sorrowful repentances of misspent lives.

Vidor of Tazambe, a fondler like myself, whose goonga proved unresponsive, reveals something of significance. She has seen our fibrillances hit the silver human carapaces and crumble, leaving only dents. And she has seen our fibrillances strike and shatter the clear bubbles of their heads. A controversy over strategy arises. Some believe it best to trim back the goonga's four snouts so that they will grow back branched, and do so again, bringing to sixteen the weapons provided by each, and in this way increase the chances of striking the clear bubbles of the enemy. But others fear that the firepower going to each fibrillance will be diminished beyond effectiveness. They prefer a radically different tack: amputate all but one snout and infect the goongas with lungmites. These will kill the goongas in two years' time, but in the interim the goongas' lung capacity will quadruple, and the firepower of the single fibrillance will be prodigious. This scheme draws equal controversy; it will be half a year before the goongas see service, and the war is now. A compromise is achieved, a long-range battle plan formalized. Our droves will begin a great retreat that is not retreat, a wide circle through many territories, each containing goongas tended differently. In the last—in the Mad Steppes abutting the Shaglands of Ordorn—the great mite-ridden one-snouted goongas will be left to mature. And if the war still rages when we complete our circle, they will be our final weapons, and the Mad Steppes our last stand.

Seated on the root of a zigzag tree, dissatisfied and oppressed by its canopy of leaves, I notice and draw attention to a totally random scribble along the south edge of the nutrient glade. We trace it back for several hours to where its intelligence first waned. From that scription we identify the one who has died the second and final death. It is Batinka. Early into a fierce war we are left without a zeromaster.

I play a prominent role in a long succession of battles. When we would defend the pass at Languishing Rock in Craterspin Valley, I drug the conjuremasters with weirdclover so that they summon up sandscrews and rockleeches instead of goongas. At Misty Crevice and Dire Canyon east of the Running Forest, it is the goongas that I drug, so that they rise indifferent to all caresses. On the pebbled plains of Skyspawn I sneeze in such a fashion that my fellows mistake it as the signal, while the enemy is yet a thousandflop distant. And in the Desert Crystallith I gather woppingglows and rig their release at the direst moment, so that the goongas about to discharge do not, but instead flee before the wild-flicker.

I am tormented by my actions and the slaughter they bring upon my kind. We are now too distant from the Evernight; those who die are denied the second life. Yet I do it. I do it and watch in horror as my love for Loud Giant is tenfold increased by each slinkie falling before her. For I see this as an expression of her supreme devotion to the memory of Awakener. And if I would have so great a lover, I must show an equal devotion.

It is said that prolonged anxiety speeds up the maturational processes. This must be so, for though barely a tripleyear in age, I spontaneously bud a son in the saltspray of Weeping Meadow. I name him Spont and send him away with the wounded, to be educated by the eminent linguist Zalsor, who was my mentor. It is my hope that he will not see any part of the war.

We, the surviving, combine many of our diminished droves and complete the outward swing of our great circle. The occasion is marked by a crushing defeat near the Shaddocks of Trite. Our drove lags and does not arrive till after the battle is lost. The southern Evernight is but a day's journey farther; there is hope of a second life for those who have perished here. Thus are we deadgathering in the hour of the echo-cloud when the swogboles all about lift their fiery sheaths to a faint whisper. In another instant we shudder before prodigious booms; everywhere slinkies fall. The enemy is upon us. I have been fondling a goonga as part of the guard detail, keeping it ever at the ready. Now the conjuremaster commands us to our task. The pointers load and aim at five charging humans. The foremost figure is tall, with red tassels nearly filling her clear bubble. It is Loud Giant. Too late do I try to undo my work; here the goongas are oversensitive, and even now mine discharges. I look on in horror as the onrushers falter together as if over a tripvine—all but one. Loud Giant charges onward, grim with the memory of Awakener. For an instant I watch the pointers fleeing to either side and wonder if perhaps they miss her intentionally, and if I am not alone in my abiding love for her. But if this is so, they do not plan as carefully as I—I, who am like the zeromaster in my determination, and who must certainly have a drop at least of that royal blood. They will not purchase her love. They will not.

I slap the goonga and whine melodiously to warn it of danger. It slips down through doughy humus, sending up to me slow bubbles like soft goodbyes. I am struck by the thought that the goongas may be as capable of loving slinkies as I am of loving a human. Beside me the conjuremaster tries to flipflop away but is wounded and cannot. Humans are charging from all sides now, but none so fast as Loud Giant. It is at this moment that I accept the invisilance through the spewovum that kills me.

There is a way by which Manuscriptors can read each other's works. In the deepnight, when the squab's control is least, the slinkie mind can use the squab's keen sense of smell to locate and trace another's path. This is how I am able to follow the war. Those now joining our ranks in the nutrient glade reveal to us that it goes ever worse. Indeed, we learn that adjacent wildglades are being tamed to accommodate our growing numbers. Renderings of each successive battle come to us. Most are so richly embroidered that we cannot believe any portion of them. Some are detailed accounts of atrocity and defeat and cannot be doubted. There are those who would have us believe that Loud Giant is dead. I will not believe this. I refuse to believe this.

We read of catastrophe at Tumbler's Heap, where the goongas are plentiful but the fibrillances misplaced; of Peninsula Sway, where the downdraft of a human airship distorts the groundwaves so that the pointers miss their targets; of Lesser Emberdusk, where a hundred slinkies discover that the goongas have chosen the direst moment for their unfathomable bedrock migration. . . .

The seasons come and go in this fashion until there arrive upon our banks (we sense rather than see) a great many slinkies. One flipflops down beside me, and I realize it is Spont, my son. He writes in the nutrient, and soon I read of the completion of the circuit and the fierce battle of Ordorn, where our kind makes its final stand. The monstrous one-snouted goongas prove formidable weapons. The lungmite infection has impressed upon their systems the need to survive, to reproduce. The slightest touch brings discharge; the slightest wait reenables it. The fibrillances thus impelled know no obstacle; they split trees, shatter rocks, and kill humans. Many, many humans. The battle of Ordorn ends with the humans repulsed, the pods returning to the sky, and the three dashing stars winking out. The battle of Ordorn is the end of the war.

The slinkies have let me read of it first, knowing that it was my painted leaf that set the stage for the war. I suspect that most of them know also of my afterwish. And I wonder . . . There is a scent about my son that is not entirely slinkie; he carries a wild squab. This he places next to me and we touch. I am ecstatic. My slinkie friends have honored my afterwish, for Loud Giant lives the second life beside me.

I worry that it will not work out between us. A squab, after all, is very particular when choosing a lifelong mate. Even now the squab that holds Loud Giant glides away. It will take time, I reassure myself. Such things take time.

We suffer a new crisis with the war's end. Batinka's final prophecy now stands satisfied. The future stretches before us like the Evernight. Though we barely skirt its edge, already we are lost. We need someone to direct us. We need, alas, a new zeromaster. Finding one is never easy. They are a rare breed—the blindly irrational, the incorrigibly ignorant. The ones who seldom read another trail . . . the solitary minds that wander alone . . . incessant, introverted scribblers . . .

Upon a time we sought the rule of erudites, but such was their openmindedness that they could not choose a clear path for us. We floundered through the centuries, victims of uncertainty, till we tried zeromaster rule. A zeromaster must be brilliantly ignorant. A zeromaster will not hesitate to point us in a wrong direction. We then need only to take the opposite way.

We have a new zeromaster at last. It is, of course, Loud Giant. But there is a problem. Her language is not ours, and while the human spoken language comes easily to us, that which they write does not fit our minds. Four of our greatest living linguists gather to study the human documents we have gathered from the war. Zalsor, my onetime mentor and now my son's, heads the group. One member soon grows so distressed at the difficulties that he kills himself. Zalsor herself will do likewise at a later time, but with great magnanimity. The language is slowly, painstakingly learned, and there comes a day when Zalsor deems the linguists ready. They descend to read the zeromaster's solitary scrawl and find it entirely incomprehensible.

The seasons roll onward, and though the war has ended, we remain in turmoil, for we do not know our direction.

It is again the Painting Season, the time to appeal to nature for improvements in its attire. I can no longer participate, being a Manuscriptor of the Evernight, but my son can, and he carries on my quest for a better zigzag leaf. He brings his leaf to me before going to the festival. He puts it in the path of my squab so that the latter must crawl over it. In this way I sense its structure and hue. It is nothing like mine. My son does not appreciate my orange tints, my gray flecking of the edges, or the symmetry of my venation. Instead he goes for tinseled edging, fine close-set stripes that distort with knots along their length, and an intricate asymmetrical venation like that in rampoid eyes.

His leaf is better.

I scribe that he should return to tell me of the festival. This he does, but he does not come alone. The banks are heavy with slinkies, and we, the Manuscriptors of Evernight, read of the festival with shock. No awards are given this year because Zalsor, our foremost linguist, lifts a baby goonga, arouses it, and takes three shafts in the invidex. She does it for the good of all, in the hope that as a Manuscriptor she will know the zeromaster's scribble, for we must learn our path.

It is a week before Zalsor acclimates and resumes her work in Evernight. Wherever we scent Loud Giant's passage, Zalsor's soon follows. And then there comes a day when Zalsor scribbles a translation:

"My kind will not give up! More will come. More, and still more! And they will slaughter every last one of you!"

The message reaches us in different ways. Those on the bank, those in the first life, see it immediately; we of the Evernight must read the scribble one by one. But eventually we all know. And at the news, we rejoice.

I must now stop writing. The day draws to an end, and Loud Giant approaches. I think at last she wants me to go with her deep into the mating cove, where we will squirm together, unsheathed, like two humans on a soft-soil mound.

Here is a powerful, deeply moving story about monstrosities, physical, emotional and musical.

FUGUE

BY WILLIAM KNUTTEL

Mary Tavan fumbled with her rosary, waiting for noon Mass to begin. She twisted around to gaze at her six-year-old son, Daniel, who sat at the synth-organ in the choir loft behind her. His silhouette seemed dim and distant, lost in the bright rays of sun shining through the stained-glass windows of the clerestory.

"Henry," she said, "do you think Daniel will be all right?"

"Of course, Mary." He smiled. "Stop worrying—he'll do fine."

Mary knew it might be Daniel's last performance for a long time. She watched him nervously shuffle the sheet music on the synth-organ music stand with his enlarged right arm. His left arm stretched toward one of the pitted, obsolete pipes from the church's original organ; electricity had replaced compressed air long, long ago. She could not see his oversized right leg behind the coving of the organ loft, but she imagined that Daniel must have it resting on the pedal board at some impossible angle. She hoped he was comfortable.

"Mary!" Henry whispered. "Father Corson is about to begin Mass."

Mary turned toward the candlelit altar, then took Henry's mutilated right hand, her body pushing against the fluffy white goat's wool of his sweater. With his good hand, Henry held the hymnal open to the introit, which bore the title "Be praised, my Lord, with all Thy creatures. Text by St. Francis. Music by Daniel Tavan."

The priest entered in a swirl of red-and-gold vestments. As his foot touched the first of the three marble steps to the altar, Daniel struck the opening chords. The altar boys knelt behind the priest, their simple black robes draping and covering their legs. The priest gestured to the life-sized statue of Christ that hung behind the altar, his hands waving in time to the Latin.

After Daniel played through the melody once, the chorus and multitude began to sing. Mary looked at her husband, then joined in: *"Laudato si, me Signore, cum tucte le tue creature. . . ."* She jabbed Henry in the side, prompting him to sing, but he continued muttering to himself, something about *"andante cantabile."*

As Daniel sustained the final chord, a throbbing minor triad, everyone knelt for the Mass's opening prayer. Henry, red-faced, hesitated and was left standing. Mary tugged at his slacks, pulling him down.

"Don't be so hard on the boy, Henry. You know how much pain he's in."

"He's embarrassing us, Mary. He's playing like a novice."

Daniel Tavan had a genetic defect. The entire right side of his body was growing out of control. The symptoms had appeared over the course of a year: first pain and muscular hypertrophy, but then more certain signs of deformation as the process accelerated. Daniel was no longer symmetric. He was dying from growing pains.

The Tavans had taken Daniel from one physician to the next, from specialist to specialist, until finally the research facility at the University Medical Center was their only hope. Dr. Silvey, a pediatrician specializing in genetics, suspected an enzyme defect related to gene coding, and he was directing research in that area.

Something had triggered a malfunction in Daniel's genes. Henry had a sneaking suspicion that the doctors had screwed up when his genetic material had been altered. Mary, her religious beliefs goading her into guilt, was sure something had happened during the test-tube gestation. Dr. Silvey disagreed with both of them. The chances for a genetic defect were much greater, he insisted, when the mother was thirty-nine and the father was forty-three. He even hinted that the stress and strain of Henry's accident, which had occurred a year before the conception, might have affected Henry's genetic material.

Dr. Silvey was waiting for Daniel and his parents when they arrived at the Medical Center. He led Daniel into the examination room and lifted him onto the table. "How's this brave young man doing today?"

"It hurts," Daniel replied. The words came from the left side of his mouth, as if the bloated right side had swollen shut.

"Let's lay you down." The doctor braced Daniel's misshapen head and back with his arm. He poked and pressed various points along Daniel's body. "Where does it hurt?"

"Everywhere. It just hurts."

The doctor turned to Mary and Henry, who waited patiently near the doorway. "Has he complained of pain more often than before?"

Mary nodded. "The last week has been very bad."

"Understandable," Dr. Silvey said. "His bone and musculature are developing so fast that he has pain simply from the increased tension. It's time for something more than sedatives." He turned to Daniel. "I have to talk to your mom and dad for a few minutes, Daniel. The nurse will come check your temperature; you can tell her about your church recital, okay?"

The doctor called his nurse in, then motioned for Mary and Henry to follow him to his office.

"I received the results from the latest tests," the doctor said, tapping his pen on the desk. "My suspicion has been confirmed: Daniel's problem is inactive symmetrase. My colleagues and I agree there is only one regimen to follow. Since we can't induce formation of symmetrase, we'll have to introduce the enzyme into Daniel's cells externally. A number of agents are available for transporting large molecules across cell membranes, and we've chosen the most suitable one."

"Will the treatment be dangerous?" Mary asked.

"Mrs. Tavan, we're working at the frontiers of medical knowledge. Yes, the risk is great. We've never worked with symmetrase *in vivo,* and we don't have time to do any preliminary work. Your son's life is at stake."

Mary slumped into her chair. "Is there any chance that the process could stop as quickly as it started?"

"It's not anything I would count on. Daniel is deforming rapidly."

"For God's sake," Henry interrupted, "we can't let Daniel get any worse than he already is. We've got to do something. Daniel is a prodigy. If we don't do something now, his talents will be just as wasted as"—he held up his mutilated hand for her to see—"as mine! He'll be just another freak!"

"Henry, it's his life we're worried about! His training as a musician doesn't enter into it."

"But he was *bred* to be a musician, Mary. It's his greatest love."

"Only because you drive him to it. It's always another lesson, another recital." She turned to Dr. Silvey. "I suppose we don't have much choice but to put Daniel through the treatments."

"I'm afraid not, dear," Henry said.

"Can you describe the treatments?"

"Daniel will be injected with the symmetrase solution intravenously, until we've determined that his cells have taken up a sufficient quantity of active enzyme. Most of the risk comes after that. Different types of cells may not respond in an identical manner. If they don't, we'll deal with problems as they arise. But if all goes well, he'll need a lot of your attention in the next few months."

"I can cut down my teaching load," Henry said. "There are other keyboard players in the area who would be willing to take on my students. And Mary has already requested a leave of absence from her job. We'll have plenty of time to take care of Daniel."

Henry closed the frayed second volume of Spitta's *Johann Sebastian Bach* and slid it onto the maple coffee table. Mary heard the cracking sound from his knees as he leaned forward.

"Haven't you read that book before?" she asked.

"Many times. And I want to read it many times more."

Henry got up and went to the organ. It was an old, reconditioned electronic console, complete with all the stops and combinations of full baroque registration. Henry had inherited the organ from his great-grandfather. The numerous keyboards were terraced in a teak-veneered cabinet, with controls for tone color on either side. As he stroked the keys with his mutilated hand, Mary sensed Henry's despair. She pitied him; she often questioned God's decision to interfere with his livelihood, his dedication to music.

Henry moved his hand over the keys in a glissando. "I think Daniel should start his lessons again. Now."

Mary glanced away. "You promised the lessons could wait until I felt he was ready."

"Didn't the doctor say he should pursue as normal a life as possible?"

"Henry, don't you understand? The treatments seem to have checked the disease, but there's still something wrong. He wants to say things, but all that comes out is advanced baby talk. I think he needs time to relearn, to become the precocious child he once was."

"Dr. Silvey is sure there's been no change in his mental capacity," Henry said. "Have you seen the compositions he's scribbled lately?"

She shook her head.

"I have, Mary. I've"—he looked at his hands—"played them, as best I could. And they're wonderful. They're not Bach, or Buxtehude, but . . . they're Daniel. He has something to say, whether he puts it into words or not."

Mary sighed. "He's asked me about the organ. A couple of times. Will you promise me you'll go easy on him? That you won't push him?"

"Of course, Mary."

"He may not have very good control of his right hand yet. That's what worries me. It could hurt him more than help him."

"I understand, dear." He kissed her, a quick peck on the cheek.

When Mary returned to the music room with Daniel, she stopped in surprise at the doorway. Henry was sitting at the organ, tracing the notes of a melody. Daniel's body tensed at the sight and sound of the organ, but Mary held his head to her hip to keep him quiet. She ran her hand through the blond hair that remained on the bloated right side of his head and watched Henry's attempt to regain the lost magic. But she knew that missing fingers meant missing notes. The melody was hollow and incomplete.

"Henry?" Mary asked.

He turned, folding his arms over his chest. To hide his inadequate hand, she thought.

Daniel smiled at his father, using the half of his mouth that could still be turned into a smile.

"Would you like to play, Daniel?" Henry asked.

Daniel nodded and went to the organ. His gait was uneven, his body rotating around the malformed right leg in an exaggerated limp.

Daniel watched with wide eyes as Mary helped to position him on the bench. He straightened his head and back as much as possible, but the lopsided neck prevented him from achieving balance. He wore corduroy jeans and a flannel shirt. Mary had fabricated them from the two halves of separate sets of clothes.

Henry reached to the bookshelf behind the organ and pulled out some of the manuscripts Daniel had produced in the last few months. He chose one and put it on the music stand. Daniel's eyes crossed slightly as he looked at Henry.

"Can play?"

"Yes, son. Try one that you've written. We can have other lessons later."

Various purring and squealing sounds came from the organ as Daniel adjusted the registers with his left hand and tapped at keys gingerly with his right. Henry frowned as the texture and timbre of the sound wandered, but soon Daniel had the baroque tone color he wanted. Mary watched Henry intently and saw a dreamy look on his face as Daniel formed the first phrases of the composition, very slowly, very methodically.

"Your rhythm is off, Daniel. And you should concentrate on balancing the melodies between hands," Henry said when Daniel had finished the piece. "Let's try another one." Henry put a yellowed copy of a Bach fantasia on the music stand.

Daniel had played the piece before. Mary, who had been watching with trepidation, relaxed when Daniel seemed more confident. After he had played the opening measures, he closed his eyes and tilted his head back.

"Daniel!" Henry grabbed Daniel's arms. "You're slurring the counterpoint. You're—" Henry released Daniel's arms and sat down on the bench beside him. "I think," he said, evenly, "we should begin some exercises."

"I think Daniel should rest now," Mary interrupted.

"Let's ask the boy, Mary. Daniel, would you like to play some more?" He rested his hand on Daniel's shoulder.

Daniel, who had not been paying attention, stopped toying with the keys and looked up. "I play. Fun!"

Father Daugherty wore a traditional robe, replete with small black buttons (from the pearl-white collar down to the hem that dragged on the floor) and black-on-black embroidery. In the rectory's austere vestry he pulled two black fiber-glass chairs from the window and gestured for Mary to sit down.

"We miss Daniel's recitals very much, Mrs. Tavan," he said.

"Believe me, Father, he misses them as much as anybody. He spends entire days at the organ." Mary glanced out the window to the convent beyond. "It worries me, Father. It may be too much for him."

"Have you gotten your doctor's opinion?"

"Of course. He's very optimistic about the treatments. The assay for symmetrase activity has remained stable for three months now, and Dr. Silvey thinks the best medicine for Daniel is to keep him occupied."

"But you don't agree?" Father Daugherty's brow was furrowed, and a lock of his stiff white hair dropped across the wrinkles.

"No. I worry that he still can't speak like he used to."

"I thought Daniel's speech problems began before the treatments—that they actually coincided with the onset of his disease."

Mary turned toward the window, avoiding Father Daugherty's eyes. Nuns were marching a group of children in the newly mown field. Their steps kicked up fresh green clumps of grass.

"Mrs. Tavan, there is obviously something more you wanted to see me about."

She continued staring. Her eyes scanned beyond the convent, regarding the puffy pillows of clouds against the azure. "It's my husband," she said. "He makes Daniel work so hard. I think he wants Daniel to replace what was taken from him."

Father Daugherty crossed his legs, smoothing the material of his robe with his hands. "Your husband is a stern man, a bitter man. I've often wondered whether my oath to God would remain strong if He decided to take as much from me as he did from your husband."

Mary pinched her lower lip with her teeth. "He remembers the master musician he was, and it makes him feel like a freak. He can't accept Daniel, because Daniel is a freak, too. Except that Daniel may still have the ability to do what Henry cannot . . . so he pushes and pushes and pushes." Mary's voice dropped to a whisper. "I watch what he does during Daniel's lessons, but when I question him about it he denies his own actions. I don't know if I can excuse him much longer."

"Then you must stop the lessons."

Mary shook her head. "I can't do that, Father. The only time Daniel seems happy is when he plays the organ."

Father Daugherty leaned back in his chair. "You need help, Mrs. Tavan. Could the three of you come see me? Perhaps he would be more reasonable."

Mary sighed, then nodded. "I'll ask him, Father."

Daniel played the first few measures of a toccata, stopping where Henry had indicated.

"Not quite, Daniel. These notes," Henry said, pointing, "these notes are *fortissimo*. The phrase is a *decrescendo*. Try it again, okay?"

Daniel nervously brought his hands to the keyboard. The first chord of the toccata thundered in a staggered sequence, culminating in a rapid succession of melodic fragments. Daniel stumbled through the notes again.

"Stop! Stop right there. It is *fortissimo*. Don't you understand? Play it again!"

Daniel stared at his father, eyes peeping out from his misshapen face. He grabbed his father's disfigured hand and squeezed, pulling his father closer. His face was expressionless.

"Daniel, what do you want?" Henry asked. He pulled back, but Daniel held him firmly. "Let me go, Daniel. I'm your father. Respect me!"

"We play something else," Daniel said, very quietly.

Henry tugged harder.

"New song," Daniel continued.

Henry nodded slowly. "Yes. New song."

Daniel released his grip.

"I'm home, dear." Mary walked into the kitchen and set a heavy bag of groceries on the table.

Henry leaned against the ceramic counter near the sink. A half-eaten sandwich lay on a stoneware plate. He rubbed his swollen hand.

The sounds of a fugue, distant and muffled, vibrated through the house. The music room was at the opposite end of the hall.

"He's playing beautifully," Mary said.

Henry stared at the Spanish mosaic tiling of the floor. "He's getting worse."

Mary frowned. "Are you all right?"

"He hurt me, Mary. He's strong. Just plays. He doesn't pay attention to technique."

"How did he hurt you?"

"He grabbed my bad hand and wouldn't let go."

"Were you reprimanding him?"

"Of course not. I never do. He just grabbed me."

"I spoke to Father Daugherty today. I think the three of us should go see him."

Henry looked up. "What can *he* do? This is a medical problem! There's something wrong with Daniel!"

"Henry, *you're* the problem! Daniel can't learn that fast."

"Don't tell me how to teach. I've been teaching music for twenty-five years!"

"But Daniel isn't like one of your former students, Henry. Don't you see that?"

"Yes, he's different. Once he was a prodigy, but now he's a monster. We should take him back to the doctor, Mary. Soon."

They argued the rest of the evening, but Mary could not persuade him to see Father Daugherty. She slept poorly that night, and made up her mind to see Dr. Silvey in the morning—about Henry, not Daniel.

Mary glanced at Dr. Silvey as the taxi stopped in front of the Tavan residence. "Thank you for agreeing to see Henry."

Dr. Silvey smiled. "Glad to do it, Mrs. Tavan. It's part of my job to counsel the patient's relatives as well as the patient."

They got out of the cab. As Mary paid the fare, they heard the sound of the organ.

"Another lesson," she muttered.

They walked across the lawn to the front door. Mary fumbled with the keys. "That doesn't sound like Daniel playing."

"Henry?" the doctor asked.

"Definitely not Henry, either."

Mary recognized bits and pieces of melodies, but the recital was a mishmash of toccatas, preludes, chorales, canzoni and fugues. Notes swirled and tumbled with each other, sometimes melodious but mostly dissonant, arrhythmic, cacophonous. She pushed the front door open.

"Make yourself comfortable, Dr. Silvey. I'll see where Henry is."

As Mary walked down the hall, purse still in hand, she noticed something about the music: it repeated the same sequence of notes every half-minute or so. She opened the door to the music room.

. "Daniel? What are you—Henry!"

Henry was slumped on the floor, at the base of Daniel's bench.

"Daniel! Daniel, what happened?"

Daniel continued playing his piece, rocking in a slow revolution each time the tune was repeated. "Again. Again. Again," he intoned.

"Daniel, stop it!" Mary grabbed his huge right arm. "Stop playing. What happened?"

Daniel ignored her. She cut the power to the organ. He turned to her, yielding; she took him to his room.

When she returned, Dr. Silvey was crouched over Henry. "He's dead, Mrs. Tavan."

"My God, no." She knelt over Henry's body, taking his limp hand in hers. "How?"

"Perhaps a heart attack, or a cerebral hemorrhage. I can't tell for sure."

Mary ran her hand through Henry's hair, kissed his hand. It was his deformed hand; there was a bruise around the wrist. She shivered.

Daniel withdrew, spoke less than ever. He avoided the organ, refused to go to the music room. At Mary's request, Dr. Silvey ran a new battery of tests.

"His responses to the raw intelligence tests are as strong as ever," he reported to Mary on the day before the funeral. "There's been a slight decrease in symmetrase activity, and it seems that some additional growth has occurred. But the changes are slight. The best indicator is that he doesn't seem to be in any pain."

Mary was relieved, but she still felt uneasy when Daniel stared at her. She tried to explain the funeral ceremony to him, but he did not seem to understand.

At the funeral, Mary, Daniel, and Father Daugherty sat in the front pew. The altar overflowed with poppies, carnations, lilies and roses, but Mary did not notice their fragrance.

When Father Corson began the services, the organ player struck the first towering notes of the final section of Bach's *The Art of Fugue*. Mary had chosen the piece as a tribute to Henry's lifework and love: it was his favorite composition. The clavier fugue was only a fragment, two hundred and thirty-nine bars long. It introduced three different themes and ended, incomplete, at the point where the three themes combined. Bach had died before completing the composition, and Mary could not help seeing the parallel with the interruptions of Henry's own career, first as a performer, then as a composer and teacher.

Six pallbearers carried the casket, entering from the rear of the church and proceeding down the center aisle. They followed a red carpet to the altar. Each pew had a single rose tacked to the end.

Daniel sat near the aisle, wearing a hastily and awkwardly assembled suit. When the casket came into view, he tugged at Mary's arm and asked, "Does Dad love me?"

Mary stared at him for a moment. She stooped and kissed his cheek. "Of course he did, Daniel. He loved you very much."

Daniel shook his head. "Dad loves music."

"Yes, Daniel, he did. But not as much as he loved you."

The casket neared the altar. The fugue was only minutes away from its terrible, glaring abyss, when Mary felt Daniel move away from her.

"Daniel!"

She began to follow him, but Father Daugherty restrained her. "Stay here, Mrs. Tavan. I'll see to the boy."

Mary closed her eyes and prepared for the jolt, the wrenching feeling she had always associated with the fugue's death notes.

But the fugue died prematurely, with a collage of chaotic notes, and voices.

"Let me go!" said a voice from above.

"No! He loves music. *My* music!"

Mary spun around and looked up to the organ loft. Daniel was sitting at the synth-organ. The organist was standing to one side, rubbing his arm.

Daniel struck a few introductory notes, then played one of the themes of the fugue, then the next, and the third, until he had reached the point where it had been interrupted. The themes began to mesh.

Mary, caught between elation and panic, turned toward the casket and again poised herself for the jolt.

But the fugue thundered on. The melodies swirled in and around each other, coalescing and then wandering, finding unity and yet remaining distinct.

Mary bowed her head, relaxing in the power of the music. She felt Bach, she felt Henry. The melodic lines were firm, and even, and vibrant.

It was Daniel's music.

This story, in a curious way, mingles the themes of The
Flying Dutchman *and Heinlein's "Universe"—a wind-pow-
ered "generation ship," sailing the seas forever.*

*The title, of course, is from Jane Taylor's "Twinkle, Twin-
kle, Little Star," which has the distinction of being the only
poem parodied by Lewis Carroll that is better known today
than the parody.*

UP ABOVE THE WORLD SO HIGH

BY MARIO MILOSEVIC

Anny sang wherever she wanted to. On deck, belowdecks, it
didn't matter.

"Why do you sing?" I asked her once. She looked at me
strangely. "Why does anyone sing, Camille?"

"I don't know," I said.

So she took me to the topmost deck. Fifty feet or more above
the waves, with the masts rising even higher, wavering and sliding against the pink sky. I looked at my feet to keep from getting
dizzy.

"Now *listen,*" she whispered.

The ship creaked. Chickens clucked and goats bleated from the
stern. Faint rumblings came from the decks below.

I didn't hear what she wanted me to hear. The ship: that was
all I knew or cared about. But Anny knew something more. She
was topside almost every chance she could get. She listened to the
wind and the ocean; then she tried to imitate them with her
songs.

I miss Anny a lot now. I even miss her songs that I never
understood. That time on the deck, she tried so hard to show me.
She made me close my eyes, made me concentrate on the water.

Then she started humming. Very faintly at first, getting louder
and louder, until she was as loud as the wind.

"Now do you see? The ocean is telling me something. It's
telling us all something if only we'd listen."

I nodded. But she could see I was only trying to be nice.

"Do you realize there is a lot more to the world than this
ship?" she asked.

"*World* is big. Without it we couldn't survive."

"*World* is a big boat, but just a boat. We can't live here forever,
and someday we'll have to land. We've only lasted this long because many of us died in the first big storm and we were able to
stretch our supplies for years."

"If we leave *World* we die," I said. "That's the truth."

I guess if you had to call Anny anything, it would have to be a
dreamer. She got a job on mast and sail maintenance, once. It
was dangerous work, but she was small and could scamper
around the masts and get into tight places a lot easier than many
others. I think that was where she learned so much about the
ocean. "The boat is so tiny," she told me. "You can see it moving
up and down on the water. At times I feel so small. It's like this
huge ocean is going to swallow up *World* and everyone on it."

She even stayed out during storms. I can still picture her hanging on to the sails, buffeted by the violent winds and rains and
singing her songs. The first time she did that, she came to my
room afterward. She was shivering and her long hair clung to her
shoulders. "Do you have a blanket?"

"Anny! What have you done to yourself?"

She smiled. "Nothing."

I pulled her from the door and helped her out of her wet
clothes.

Anny was a year older than I, but my fourteen-year-old body
was much more developed than hers. She was so thin! "What's
wrong with you?" I asked. "Are you sick?"

She covered herself with my blankets. "Nothing. I'm fine."

"Have you been eating?"

"You're not my mother. Leave me alone."

"I'm worried about you."

"Please, Camille. Will you get me something hot to drink?"

I made some tea for her. I had to use what was left of my week's ration, but I didn't mind. Anny was my friend.

"What were you doing?" I asked.

When she told me, I refused to believe her. My parents had told me about the storm that carried away all our small craft and killed a lot of people on board, including the captain and most of the crew.

"No one could survive that," I said. "You'd be blown off the rigging."

"Nevertheless," she said, "that *is* what I was doing. You can believe me or not, I don't care."

Maybe she had a death wish. She certainly believed her life was not worthwhile aboard *World*. Only during a storm did she feel part of the world she wanted so terribly much. But it was a world she could never have. I told her so.

"Camille," she answered, "some people don't belong in the time and place where they are born. I should have been born when *World* was first setting out. Then we were full of the spirit of adventure. Now it's all gone, and we can never get it back. Sometimes that makes me so sad. You laugh at my songs—"

"No! I just—"

"Don't. I understand, I am a comical figure. You laugh at my songs, but sometimes my songs turn to tears, and if you heard me then you wouldn't laugh."

She wept, and I held her thin body close. I felt I could smother her if I held her too tight. "It'll be all right," I said. "After you're all warm and dry you'll feel much better." She sighed deeply, and I couldn't tell if it was from exasperation or contentment.

Harry, Anny's boss, soon found out she was climbing the masts at night and fired her. He didn't want any deaths on his crew, he said. It didn't stop her, though, and I even went with her once.

We waited until dark, when most of the ship was asleep. I slipped out of my room very quietly so as not to wake my parents and met Anny two decks above, near the library.

I greeted her cheerfully, but she shushed me. We went up to the topmost deck, where the cold chilled us. I looked up. We were right beside the mainmast, but even on that clear night, with a full moon shining, the mast climbed much farther than my eye could follow. The sails hung limply from the yards. The night was still. Anny swung a length of rope.

"I swiped this from Harry," she said.

I nodded.

The lowest yard was more than twenty feet above us. Anny expertly threw her rope over it—there was a weight attached—and we used it to help us scamper up the mast, which was a good six or seven feet in diameter, almost impossible to climb any other way. I didn't know rope climbing, but Anny showed me how to use my feet, one over the other, with the rope between them and around my thigh. She was very patient with me.

When we reached the yard I rested, catching my breath while she pulled the rope up. The mainsail hung like a great weight below us. There was barely a ripple in it from top to bottom.

"Ready?"

Anny had already stood up, and was hanging on to the bottom of the topsail, which hung above us, even bigger than the mainsail. From the way she stood so confidently, I guessed she didn't need to hang on to anything. I loved *World*. It was my ship as much as it was Harry's, or my parents', or even Anny's. But there were some parts of it I preferred to just look at, not experience.

"I'm not sure, Anny. Maybe this isn't such a good idea."

"Don't be afraid, I'm here. I'll look after you."

I didn't want to admit to fear, so I agreed. "Let's go," I said.

There were ratlines the rest of the way. I think it took us a good hour to get to the top, with Anny leading the way, constantly looking down to see how I was doing. We stopped for me to rest at each yard.

I didn't notice the swaying of the ship until we had passed the skysail and had crawled inside the crow's nest. Anny was hardly even breathing hard but I was sprawled on the deck unable to move. I could see her hair swaying very slowly, and it took me a minute to realize the motion was caused by the ship moving back and forth.

"We're moving, Anny! We're moving!"

"Of course we're moving. That's the rocking of the waves. It goes on all the time."

"But—"

"Down below you don't feel it so much because you are too close to the waves. But where we are now, the motion is amplified by the length of the mast. Up here you *know* you're on the ocean."

"I don't like it," I said. "I think I'm getting sick."

There was about six feet of mast extending past the crow's nest into the sky. I watched as it swung against the stars and my stomach followed the motion with a heavy sensation that wanted to crawl up my throat into my mouth.

"Don't look at the mast," said Anny. "That's what's making you sick."

"Uh-huh," I managed.

Now she started giggling. "Camille, close your eyes, dammit." She put her hand over my face, and I felt better.

"Thank you," I said, feeling foolish. After a few seconds: "You can take your hand away now." She sat against the bulkhead, facing me.

"Yours is probably the first case of seasickness aboard the *World* in a very long time," she said, grinning.

"Hilarious."

"But never mind," she said, suddenly serious. "It's good to get that out of your system." I closed my eyes, feeling the sweat begin to evaporate from my body. I don't know how long I was there, lying peacefully, oblivious of the night around me. Eventually I became aware of Anny humming a song. It was one I'd heard her sing before. It went like this:

> Twinkle, twinkle, little star,
> How I wonder what you are.
> Up above the world so high,
> Like a diamond in the sky.

"Where did you hear that song?" I asked.

"My parents used to sing it to me."

"I like it."

She shrugged. "It's too simple. Listen to this one."

Then she started singing that weird stuff again. I couldn't understand a word. It wasn't English. It just wasn't *anything*.

"Can't you sing something better?" I said.

"Do you want me to sing Twinkle-twinkle-little-star?"

"Well . . ."

"Let's look at the stars." She went to the rail and I joined her, being careful not to look down at the deck. Anny pointed out the North Star, and the Big Dipper, and Orion. She tried to show me Cassiopeia—"It's like a big 'W,' only bent a bit out of shape"— but I couldn't see it.

"Why do you like the ocean so much?" I asked.

"I don't. I hate it."

"But everything you do, the way you act—I don't understand."

"The ocean is my means of escape, nothing more."

"Where? Where can you escape to?"

"To land, Camille. That's where the future is. Not on this boat, this oversized piece of wood. It's dying. And everyone aboard it is dying."

I felt hurt. Suddenly we weren't close anymore. "I love *World*. It's my home."

"It's my home too, but that doesn't mean it can't kill me. *World* was never meant to sail the ocean forever. When the ice caps started to melt, people were turning savage and there was less and less land all the time. People built ships to get away, but we were only supposed to sail for a little while, until the danger was over on the land."

I shook my head. "No. It can't be. We'd die without this ship."

"I'm building one of my own."

"Where, how?" I felt ill again.

"I have a secret place. It's not a boat really, just a raft. But it's a good one. I steal wood from the carpentry shop and canvas from the sailmakers. I've been saving my food. I even have enough rope to lower my raft into the water when the time comes. There. I've told you everything." She looked so vulnerable that I wanted to squeeze her tight. "There's enough room and food for two people, Camille. Will you come with me?"

Her desperation only made me pity her more. "Why? Why should I? Why should you? What could you accomplish?"

What happened next I didn't understand. She started getting ready to leave. I kept asking her my question over and over, trying to get her to answer. She ignored me, pulled up the hatch and began climbing down. I followed as quickly as I could, not wanting to be left alone so high up.

But when we got to the mainsail yard she stopped. I struggled to climb beside her. "What are you waiting for?"

"We're going to go down a different way," she said.

"What way? What are you talking about?"

"When *World* first set sail the kids had a game. They would climb up here on calm days, and slide down the mainsail. It was great fun."

"How do you know what happened years ago?"

"I've read the logs. So should you. Then you'd know I'm telling you the truth about *World.* Now how about it, are you going to slide down with me?"

I tried to study her face by the moonlight, but it was in shadow. I looked at the sail past my feet. The deck was a long way down. "Have you ever done it?"

"Lots of times."

The tone in her voice told me she was lying. It wasn't that she was scared, it was like she was defying me to disbelieve her.

"What if it breaks, or tears or something?"

"It won't."

"What if a wind comes up and billows out the sail?"

"The air is calm and you know it."

"I don't know, Anny. It's a long way down, what's going to break our fall?" My palms were getting sweaty. I was sure she could feel me shivering.

"Our weight will stretch the sail so it'll make a trampoline at the bottom. The friction of our bodies against it will slow us down."

"I don't believe you. You're making all this up."

"Listen to me, Camille. You know I'm telling the truth. They really did this. They did it all the time."

"No. I won't do it. It's crazy."

She grabbed me. I jumped back, but she was too strong for me. Such a thin body, but what power! It startled me, and then it was too late.

"Hang on!" she shouted. I felt a shove and grabbed at her as I lost my balance.

That was the last thing we did together. While we were making all that noise, someone heard us and called for Harry to find out what was going on. Furious, he waited at the bottom and yelled at us that we could have killed ourselves. I was too dazed to worry about him, though. Anny just smiled.

My parents confined me to quarters for two weeks, and I couldn't see Anny. I didn't lose contact with her, though. She managed to get a letter to me disguised as a note from someone else. This is what it said:

Dear Camille:

They say I've created a nuisance and will try me as a grownup. I can't let them do that because they might find out about my raft and take it away from me. So I have to leave the ship soon. Tomorrow or the next day.

I am doing what's right. On land we can find the other ships. Spaceships they are called. The bold and the brave went on those ships to look for a better planet. We must find land. From land we can get to space. You know where I am. I want you to come with me. Please, Camille, join me.

ANNY

There was a line of little words like "dum" and "dee" at the bottom of the page that I didn't understand.

I read the letter once quickly, then put it away—and kept

taking it out every few minutes. Anny was a misfit aboard the *World*. I decided we would be better off without her. We had tried to be friends, but we were too different.

When I came to that realization, a great peacefulness fell over me. It was the same feeling as when you've cleaned up your room and everything is neat and in its place. You can rest with a clear mind. That's what I did. I fell asleep.

Anny was reported missing the next day. My parents told me about it. She had escaped from her room, probably through the ventilation shaft. Anny could squeeze through almost any hole. They searched for her for days. I knew they would never find her.

When my two weeks were up, I explored the whole ship all over again, I was so happy to be free. I could tell, somehow, that Anny wasn't on board anymore. I cried a little, once, but only a little because I knew she was where she wanted to be.

My parents were trying to get me interested in a guy they liked a lot. He lived a couple of decks below us but I thought he was boring. I didn't see him very much. Mostly I concentrated on school.

Although *World* is a big ship, it is so crowded that people tend to stay to themselves to get as much privacy as possible. I know very little about the people who live next door even. It wasn't until I started reading the ship's logs that I found out who the original captain was. Captain Tyler her name was. Or his name. It didn't say if Tyler was a man or a woman and no one I knew could tell me. Not the librarian, not my parents, not my friends. It was then that I realized how small *World* really was, how big we tried to make it by pushing off other people, making them into strangers. I felt like I needed Anny again, only this time she wasn't with me and I would never see her again.

About three months after the incident in the crow's nest, we began to sight land more and more often. No one could explain it and nobody but me seemed to be excited about it. I suppose I wondered if Anny had managed to get to one of those distant lines on the horizon. When I looked at them, I thought I could hear her songs again, clear as a cloudless sky. I begged my parents to let me go ashore. They said it was too dangerous because of wild animals and primitive people, and besides, the ship couldn't get close enough anyway.

I knew they were only scared. So was everyone else. I sat in my room and read Anny's letter. I noticed the last line again, and this time something clicked. I read the words slowly and remembered Anny humming her tune when we were in the crow's nest. Not the "Twinkle, twinkle" song but the other one that I didn't like. That song and the line in the letter were the same. The sounds were like a longing cry, a wail of despair. I closed my eyes and remembered Anny singing it.

I wanted a closer look at the shores we were passing, and I knew there was only one place for that. The next morning I climbed up to the crow's nest. I wore white clothes and shoes and even a white hat so that no one would notice me in the daylight.

I thought the thing I found in the crow's nest was only a pile of rags at first, but as I pulled myself in, one end of the pile raised itself and Anny's face, shrunken and thin, peered at me with squinting eyes.

She was even more thin than I remembered her, but she sat up and greeted me. "I was wondering how long it would take you to find me here," she said. Her voice was weak.

"I wasn't looking for you. I thought you were gone months ago."

She nodded. "Of course. That's what I wanted everyone to think."

"Even me?"

"Well . . . I wasn't sure about you. I didn't know whose side you were on. On the night that I wanted to go, I came to your room and I saw you."

"I don't remember—"

"You were asleep. But I could see that you hadn't got anything ready for our trip. You were glad to be rid of me, weren't you?"

I didn't answer.

"Anyway, I decided that was it. There was just nothing at all for me here anymore. And I went to get my raft."

"But you lost your nerve before you could do it, right?"

She laughed. The sound was dry and rasping, like an old woman's laugh. It made me flinch.

"Hardly," she said. "What happened was—what happened, was that I made the raft too big to get out. I built it in this deserted little closet room that was just big enough for me and the raft, but the door was real tiny, and, well, I just didn't allow for it." She laughed again, shaking her head. "A year's work, completely wasted. The doorframe was metal. Metal! Steel, I think. I just sat there, stunned. It would have taken a month or more to take the thing apart and find another hiding place to put it back together again."

My face was calm, but inside I was screaming. Anny had never really wanted to leave. She was as tied to this ship as any of us! Her grand dream was just a dream that she was too frightened to make real. I hated her and I hated my romanticization of her.

"What did you do?"

"I climbed up here. It was the only place I had to think things over."

"And?"

"I decided I'd been doing it all wrong. I was building a boat while I was on board a ship. That was stupid. So I've been steering the *World* myself. At night, when the automatic pilot is on, I sneak in and change the heading. The people that run this ship are dim anyway—they don't know where they're going or how to get there."

I was going to tell her how crazy she was, but she interrupted me.

"Camille, dear, there's no reason for you to not go with me. Do you see that now? Already I've brought us within sight of land many times, you must have noticed. Eventually I'll bring us close enough so we can swim ashore. Or we don't even have to swim, we can just float. You'll see, we can do it."

I looked at her shrunken body. She couldn't possibly have swum the width of *World*, let alone the miles to shore.

Why is it that things always seem better in your memory? I had thought Anny was my hero. Now that I saw her again, she was a nothing.

I couldn't stand to be with her anymore. I said, "Stay here, Anny. I'll be right back with some food. We'll get through this together. Okay?"

Her head had been tilted forward, anticipating and prompting my response, which, when it came, made her relax abruptly. "Thank you," she whispered.

When I reached the deck again I called Harry and told him where he could find Anny. I warned him to be careful with her or I'd kill him in his sleep. He laughed, but he knew I was serious.

I'm not ashamed of what I did. The only person I ever knew that wasn't satisfied with life aboard *World* turned into an emaciated animal. She sang songs but she didn't eat. She wasn't sensible, and that's what you have to be.

I still have Anny's letter and I still read that last line whenever I start to get nostalgic about the stars. It makes me laugh, now, to think of those poor souls that left this planet to go to space.

Harry was careful with Anny, and I took care of her for a while until she died. She was too weak to go on. Poor Anny had wasted all her strength on a vision that could never come true.

There is a peculiar fascination in the adventures of an innocent rogue—or, better yet, two—wandering in a forgotten world of barbarism and magic. These stories are not quite fantasy as the word is commonly used, and not quite science fiction either; they form a subgenre in which, for example, Fritz Leiber and Joanna Russ have done memorable work. To their number we now add Barbara Rausch. This story, complete in itself, is an episode from an unpublished novel.

SNOWS OF YESTERYEAR

BY BARBARA RAUSCH

The skeleton up on the crude log bunk grinned at Haston; he dropped the corner of the bearskin that had covered it as if it were white-hot. Voice stuck in his throat, heart jolting, he stumbled across the earthen floor of the dugout house to claw at his partner's sleeve and point wildly at the dead thing on the upper bed.

Garthan spun, so that his tawny hair lashed his broad jaw, then sneered, "Only old bones!" But Haston's face was a pallid mask in its frame of dark hair; he continued to stare with shock-widened eyes at the skeleton.

By the daylight that seeped through the doorway of the bothy into the earth-smelling, windowless interior, the skeleton's moldering garments, and strands of long hair still bound to the skull by a leather headband, gave it a hideous semblance of life. It lay in a mockery of repose, fleshless hands clasped over some object that lay on the sunken breast.

"I was not so wide of the mark when I mistook this place for a grave mound," said Garthan.

"But he—it—isn't *buried*," Haston protested. "He must have

come in here alive, and barred the door behind him. It stood untouched and overgrown till we set our blades to its edge and pried up the bar from its brackets. It's as if he just lay down to sleep—and never woke."

"Sick, starved, I care not. Go fetch that old mattock hanging on the wall, and we'll put him under sod."

"But there are two beds," persisted Haston, eyeing the bare slats of the lower one. "Two men. What became of the other one? There's a tale here—"

"You and your tales! One lich is enough to be burying in this raw weather; how many more would you have? Fetch the mattock."

Taking it in turns with the mattock, the partners scraped a shallow trench in the stony clearing, then returned to get the skeleton.

"Get the bearhide off," Garthan commanded. "That's too good to bury." But it took both of them to bundle the heavy, dusty pelt off the remains. Sneezing and coughing, they flung it outdoors to air, then turned back to the bunk's grisly tenant.

As he considered the skeleton, Haston found himself automatically observing, reasoning, seeking some way to make sense of the inexplicable. Somehow, he felt, Garthan's hasty assessment of sickness or starvation hardly agreed with the deliberate composure of the skeleton.

"Wake up, Slow-worm," Garthan complained. "Get hold of the bedding down there, whilst I take up this end. We'll lift the whole thing down and for Fate's sake tip it not, unless you wish to be picking him piece by piece from the floor! Together now!"

Though the partners managed the ticklish business neatly enough, the movement jolted the skeleton's poised arms and shifted the hands apart. What had been held in a grasp outlasting death now escaped from its precarious rest. Haston's startled jerk at the bedding lent the leather packet momentum; it slid from the skeleton, slipped down the ragged blanket, and fell at Haston's feet.

"Never mind it," Garthan snapped. "Let's get this done with, and the place fit to stay in by nightfall."

So Haston had to ignore the packet and get on with the bury-ing. When that was done he could steal only a moment from cleaning the bothy to pick up the object. He slid it down his tunic as his partner stood up from the hearth.

"I've got the flue cleared," Garthan said, dusting his hands on the seat of his breeches. "We can have a fire tonight; we'll need it. Tomorrow we'll cut saplings and build a shelter for the horses against the side of the bothy. And right now I want to go set some snares." He looked around the bothy thoughtfully. "Our departed friend"—he jerked a thumb in the grave's direction—"did for himself very well out here. His cookpots are still good, and those arrowheads you found will help get us venison, once I've made a bow . . ."

Garthan's tawny brows drew together as his voice slowed to a perplexed rumble. "Something troubles me—"

"No windows. Graves have no windows."

Blue gaze met gray, startled, as Haston heard the words com-ing from his own lips.

"Hold your tongue, fool," Garthan retorted, suddenly savage. He picked up his snares and crossed the bothy in three long strides. Halfway out the door he turned back abruptly. "By the time I return," he added, "you'd better have the old-wives' non-sense out of your head." Then he was gone.

For a long time Haston sat numbly on the bothy's only other furnishing, a rickety bench, his mind a welter of perturbed thoughts. Just hours ago he and Garthan had called the over-grown, moundlike bothy a gift from Fate, a snug forest sanctuary for two fugitives against the coming winter. It lay in a natural clearing, where a spring gushed from a granite outcrop, source of the stream that had led them there from the forest's edge. Before the bothy's discovery, Haston, village-bred, had been apprehen-sive of his woodsman partner's insistence on a wilderness refuge, and now those misgivings assailed him again.

At last the chill draft from the open doorway stirred him to movement. He went to close the door, pulling his tunic about him, but stopped suddenly when something prodded his ribs. He pulled the leather packet from his belt.

A little broader than his palm and a finger thick, it was a flat squarish hide pouch stitched round the edges with coarse sinew. All at once impatient, Haston drew his knife and cut the sinew ties.

The two coarse sheets of vellum he found within had been so long folded that the first one broke at a touch along the creases. Haston pieced the page together on the bench like a puzzle, then studied the scrawled characters. There was something teasingly familiar about them; oddly enough, they made him think of Garthan.

But Garthan can neither read nor write, Haston remembered. *He couldn't even learn the Twenty Runes*—With that thought came recognition, and a flash of boyhood memory: himself at his Gran'sire's feet, watching the old man mark the Runes in the earth with a stick as he named them. *Learning the Runes myself was easy,* Haston recalled. *Trying to pound them into Garthan's head was the hardest teaching I ever attempted . . .*

Haston realized that he was squinting at the markings and that evening was falling. He built a fire with the trash of their cleaning efforts, wondering a little at Garthan's long absence, but glad of the opportunity to examine his discovery uninterrupted. By firelight he read the page again.

Part of it seemed to be a hunter's tally—a list of game, animals' names followed by varied numbers of strokes to mark how many of each animal had been taken. Halfway down the page there was a date.

Pethan sixth—it's Pethan now, Haston thought, *but well past the full moon.* After the date, the writing became dense and cramped, but he puzzled out the rest of the page. There were two long passages, each headed by a date.

Pethan 6 Piars of Duuri writes this. Here is good hunting. We are three days in this wood. We take already //fox /// beaver /stoat ////hares. My partner Rahk says, let us stay this place so we get many pelts for sell. I say, soon the snow comes. Rahk says, we make earth house. When other hunters go back to Duuri we stay and take more pelts. I say,

is that not very hard. Rahk laughs and says, but then we are
greatest hunters, and get very rich. I see he will do this, with
me or without. Yet we are partners. I do not leave him alone
here in the long winter.

Pethan 22 For sixteen turns of the lamp we make the earth
house. It is deep only to my shoulder but we pile around
hole many stones we have dig up. Then we set roof poles.
Enough stone we have left for fireplace. Let snow come,
Rahk says as we lay turves for roof, we be ready. Even while
we toil, our snares take many pelts. Two days we find wolf
sign, so Rahk has make a strong door. Today I ride back to
Duuri, and bring good iron bar and hinges

The Runes blurred before Haston's aching eyes as he struggled
to finish the page. Reluctantly he put the packet away in his
saddlebag, more disturbed than enlightened by the little he had
read. When Garthan swept in, good spirits restored, he found
Haston huddled in front of the fireplace, shivering, staring at the
dying embers.

"To the Seven Hells with it, that's the third shot it's missed."
With a curse Garthan snapped the hastily made bow across his
knee. Haston sighed, weary of days of futile hunting, resigned to
a diet of small game and roots. But Garthan was savagely determined to get a deer.

"Give me the mattock," he demanded. "I'm going to set some
deadfalls on this trail. You go check the snares," he added. "I'll
see you in camp by sundown."

Dismissed, Haston turned back unwillingly. He hated collecting the snares' pathetic harvest. Finishing the distasteful duty as
quickly as possible, he hurried back to the bothy and sought out
the thing that nagged at his mind.

Until this moment Haston had found no opportunity to read
more of Piars' journal. Now he brought out the packet and carefully unfolded the second sheet of vellum. He looked first at the
dates that stood out from the crowded page. They ran, approxi-

mately, from the end of Pethan to the third week of Ruisan, the
following month.

"Still alive a month later," Haston muttered. He looked back
at the top of the page and began to read.

The first few entries were brief: game tallies and records of
intermittent and increasing snowfalls. But, halfway through the
month, the entries changed. The single tally list became two,
each headed by a hunter's name. And beneath the tallies Piars
had written several longer passages:

Ruisan 16 Always I know Rahk is greedy but now I think he
cheats me. I do not see it but I think he shifts the best pelts
from my cache to his. Then he puts in my cache his pelts
that are not good. He thinks I shall not know. From now I
keep two tallies so I can prove if he cheats me again. I am
sad. Until now he is good partner.

Ruisan 17 Today Rahk watches me make tallies. I know he
does not like that I can make and he cannot. He asks to
know why I keep two tallies now. I say, I wish not to make
mistakes. He says, what does it matter, you waste your time.
I say, perhaps so, but I wish to do it. Then he has no answer,
so he is angry. He makes a great show of putting his cache
away from mine.

Ruisan 19 Today it snows all day. Yesterday Rahk was the
whole day making a pen for the horses. He does not talk to
me. I do not talk to him. He watches me write. I think when
this page is full, I keep the tallies in my belt pouch.

Ruisan 20 It is three days that Rahk stays angry and will not
speak. It snows so much we cannot go out to the snares.
Rahk is line his tunic with rabbit hides. While I am out
yesterday I ruin my boots with damp. So now I ask Rahk to
help me make new ones. He says, tomorrow. I think he is
not so angry now. It is I who should be angry, I think.

Ruisan 21 Today it snows so hard we cannot see across the
clearing. We go out only to tend the horses. I think Rahk is
through with his anger. He does not speak of it. In my cache

I find just enough otter skins for new boots. Rahk puts on
the shelf the spike he did not need for the door and says

There the page ended, filled to the bottom on both sides. Frustrated, Haston yanked the pouch apart, though he knew it held
nothing more, and sat for a time with the torn leather dangling
from his hands. At last, aware of hunger, he mended the fire and
skinned out the day's catch of game. He had just skewered two
rabbits over the flames when the door banged open.

A rush of freezing air followed Garthan as he entered the
bothy, his hair and shoulders glittering with sleet. He struggled a
little, clumsily, with the door, then turned, and even by firelight
Haston could see the taut expression on his partner's face. Haston came to Garthan's side and took the mattock from his cold
hand.

"What's amiss?" Haston asked. For a moment Garthan was
silent, his gaze hard and remote. Then he thrust his hand into the
bag that held his hunting gear.

"Here's the other half of your tale."

Even though the harsh note in Garthan's voice warned him,
Haston was stunned; in his partner's hand was the naked visage
of death. Another skull—but the bad thing was the spike, a finger's breadth of cruel iron, its rust running like bloodstains down
the skull's violated temples and gleaming ugly red through the
staring sockets. Haston swallowed and said weakly, "No! How
can you know—"

"The spike. There are nine more just like it in the bothy door."

Haston had no need to look at the door. He remembered too
well how the massive iron fittings had stubbornly resisted their
assaults. He pulled his gaze away from the skull to meet
Garthan's.

"I was making deadfalls back down the trail," Garthan explained, "digging. It—the bones were scattered, but I picked up
what I could." His fingers fumbled at the bag. "I think we—
Shouldn't we put him with his—the other one?"

What Haston had read in the journal came back to him with
wicked irony; but he could not bring himself to cast the burden of

what he knew upon his partner. Smiling an assurance he did not
feel, Haston took the skull from Garthan's hand and put it aside
on the shelf before he replied. "Surely. First thing tomorrow.
Now, come and get warm."

Garthan paced back and forth across the bothy, swinging the
mattock. "Come along; let's finish this ere the snow's any
deeper."

Haston made no response but stood motionless, his gaze intent
on the shelf. With a long stride Garthan came to his partner, but
his impatient words died unspoken. Their gazes met, then fled to
the heap of bone fragments littered on the wood.

"Did you touch the skull?" Haston's eyes begged "yes" for an
answer, but Garthan shook his head.

"Then why is it broken now?"

"Not so strange," Garthan replied. "Pierced as it was, only the
moist clay it lay in held the skull together this long. Here, in the
drier warmth . . ."

"So. He is nothing now," Haston said in a harsh tone as he
watched Garthan gather up the shards of bone. Garthan's thick
fingers brushed the murderous iron and spurned it.

"A man is nothing—" Haston echoed himself. "But that
damned spike still remains . . ."

"Forget it." Garthan thrust the bag with its dismal burden into
Haston's hands, and pushed him toward the door.

The two made a grim little procession under the bleak sky,
their footsteps stitching a crooked black seam across the clearing.
Their breath misted the air and the cold gnawed their hands as
they labored in the frozen earth.

"Enough," Garthan grunted. Haston laid the bones, bag and
all, in the raw gaping soil at his feet. Garthan replaced the earth
and the pall of snow over it. Haston watched, hearing the clods
rattle dully on the stiff sacking, and wondered why he felt no
relief that the mystery was done with.

Silently, relentlessly, the snow sifted out of the thick-clotted
sky and swallowed the clearing in a paralyzed stillness. Inside the

bothy, Haston shut the door behind him and dropped an armful of kindling on the hearth to dry out. Garthan sat on the lower bed, watching, and his scowl deepened when the wood clattered on the stone. Haston froze, waiting for an outburst.

Garthan's glare went back to the boot he was greasing. Relieved, Haston fled up to the refuge of his bed and his book, thinking, *Unless the snow stops soon, this place may be our tomb also.* He resigned the greater share of their space to his partner; even so, Garthan's pent-up energy overwhelmed the tiny dwelling. More and more, Haston retreated into silence; yet even his retreat became a target.

"What in the Seven Hells do you find up there to do?" The angry demand rose from below. Both bunks shuddered as Garthan moved restlessly. The boot thumped to the floor.

"Thinking—" Haston said evasively.

"About what?" Garthan shot back.

Haston was at a loss to answer; he knew better than to admit to Garthan his own obsession with the fate of Piars and Rahk.

"I said, about what?"

"Oh, ah"—Haston prayed that Garthan would lose interest—"about Fate—how matters come about . . ." But even that was skirting too close to the debatable subject. His words failed and drowned in the waiting silence.

"Make sense."

Garthan's tone pricked Haston to a rush of annoyance that made him blurt the first thought that entered his mind.

"Do you never think of the night you raided my village?"

Silence. Then Garthan's voice, harsh and ironic. "Indeed! While I lay captive in Grefeld I thought of little else, because I could not understand what happened then."

"As I recall," Haston dared to reply, "you came but an inch from killing me."

"An inch is calling it wide," came the wry admission, and Haston felt a prickle of reminiscent fear. Yet, having said so much, he could neither drop the matter nor recall his words. And the next question lay already on his lips.

"Sometimes . . . I've wondered why you didn't—"

"Didn't kill you?" Garthan's voice was full of bafflement; but his next words stopped Haston's breath and made the hair rise on the back of his neck.

"I should have killed you!"

The bunk heaved. Chained to his bed by terror, Haston watched Garthan fling himself across the room and swing up the mattock. There was an instant without breath or heartbeat. Crouched like some savage, every line of his body a threat, Garthan glared at Haston. Confusion and murder warred in his blue eyes, and something Haston knew no name for, that iced his veins with horror. He lived and died in that moment. Then, though neither he nor Garthan blinked or stirred, the eye link snapped like thread breaking, and Haston breathed again.

The tension ebbed out of Garthan's body, left him staring at the mattock in his hand. He put it down at last with an awkward movement and looked on blankly as Haston mustered his watery limbs down from the bunk. Then Garthan's eyes rolled back, and he dropped like a felled tree into Haston's arms. Haston staggered as he eased the limp bulk of his partner's body to the floor.

Garthan's eyes opened at last, waveringly. As his gaze sharpened, he shook his head and struggled to sit up before Haston could restrain him.

"Just a touch of winter fever," Garthan insisted. "Better already." He pushed Haston's hand away from his brow, but not before Haston had judged its warmth normal, even a little cool. Haston's gaze met no more strangeness in his partner's face or eyes, only a reassuring impatience.

Garthan sprang up with his usual vigor. "Don't stare so," he demanded crossly, cramming his boots on. "I'm fit enough—Ah! I know what gnaws you. You were just wondering why I let you live, that time." His clear, slightly quizzical gaze met Haston's straightforwardly, and Haston realized with horror reborn that Garthan had no memory of the mattock incident at all.

It was the third day of snow. Haston lay face to the wall on his bed, turning an unresponsive back to Garthan.

"Very well, then," Garthan grumbled, at the end of his small patience. "Since you've no sickness that I can see—and I've seen my share—mope as you will. I'll not coddle you." So speaking, Garthan escaped to the few outdoor tasks the weather permitted.

Alone with his mood, Haston flogged himself with recriminations.

What folly brought me to this, he wondered. *Why could I not have seen that Garthan has a far better chance of surviving on his own? With no reward on my head, I could have gone home anytime. And now we're at each other's throats . . .* Those words brought back the memory Haston could not suppress: the vision of Garthan as he had been a day ago: mad-eyed, weapon-wielding, deadly.

He stared at the earthen wall inches from his face. But what he saw was the prison he shared with an unpredictable savage: the white smothering prison building itself inexorably about him. He saw himself wound and bound in a freezing shroud, his limbs numb, his lips dumb, his eyes stopped by a white blank more hideous than darkness.

Hope dwindled in Haston's heart to a dim point; his fear expanded into the void that remained. Yet fear brought with it a perverse vitality that sharpened his obsession as it drove the lassitude from his body.

He sat up slowly and peered into the lower bed to reassure himself that Garthan was gone. Possessed of a feverish energy, Haston threw down his cloak, his saddle blanket, and his half of the bearskin, then examined the bare log frame minutely. Not finding what he sought, he did the same to Garthan's bed, even reaching between and beneath the slats. He found only ancient dust.

Tossing the heaps of bedding back in place, Haston turned to the shelf. The few crude tin and pottery vessels upon it yielded nothing. Haston lifted the shelf from its pegs before abandoning it to pry at the hearthstones, upend the bench, and prod its joints. He even made a furtive rummage through Garthan's saddlebags. All fruitless.

Now, in a dither of panic and frustration, Haston was turning compulsively from one side of the room to the other, snatching up objects and flinging them down. Almost in tears, he pawed once more through Garthan's bedding in a final, futile search. Nothing.

There was nowhere else to look. Haston hunched on Garthan's bed, his eyes fixed on the unrevealing walls. Wearied by the turmoil within him, he sank down and buried his face in his arms.

"You let the fire go out," Garthan accused, looking in at darkness. Only silence replied. He thrust the door wider to let daylight into the bothy but stopped on the threshold. His gaze circled the disordered room, coming to rest at his bed, where Haston still lay. Garthan's annoyance receded before the prickle of some primeval instinct that came as a craving for space and light. He resisted it, forcing himself forward into the shadows. He looked down dubiously at Haston, who had not wakened at the sound of his voice. Finally Garthan knelt to the dead hearth and began to rekindle the fire.

A feeling like two icy fingers laid on the back of his neck sent cold alarms down Garthan's spine. It took him a lifetime to turn around, pulse slamming thick and slow against the deadly winter that locked his limbs. There was a glimpse of the white, drawn face of his partner, a pale shape afloat on the shadows.

Before the ice-gray glare that swept like a glacier's breath across his soul Garthan trembled but stood fast. Yet through his fear came a rush of pity; he had never seen mortal eyes so desolate.

"Haston," he breathed, and against every clamoring instinct strode forward.

"Thief! Cheat!" As he retreated, Haston flung the vicious words like knives across the space between them. Suddenly he jerked to a stop, caught by his loose sleeve on the splintered edge of the shelf. "No! No farther," he screamed, yanking at the trapped sleeve. As Garthan reached out to release it for him, Haston's flailing hand swept the shelf's surface—and swung up clenched.

The sound of rending fabric, a flash of something rust-red;

then Garthan's hand caught Haston's wrist, stopping the spike's point an inch from his own temple.

For a timeless moment the rasp of their breathing was the only sound. Then, snarling, Haston clamped his free hand to his partner's throat. As he pried at the strangling clutch, Garthan's eyes challenged the wild gray glare of Haston's and saw his death in it.

Locked in a violent embrace, the two reeled panting and cursing across the narrow room. All Garthan's savage instincts rose in a blazing tide; he flung off the choking grasp and bore his adversary back against the bunk. His thick hands circled Haston's neck; then through a mist of fury Garthan looked again at the anguished face inches from his own. Ignoring the blows that fell on his head and shoulders, he swept Haston up bodily and lunged for the doorway.

As they burst into the daylight, Haston's struggles stopped; he went limp. Garthan staggered with him toward the center of the clearing before they collapsed together in the snow.

The cold drove Garthan back to his senses, but Haston lay utterly still where he had fallen, his face hardly less white than the snow surrounding it. Garthan dragged his partner upright, shook and slapped him. Haston flinched from the blows, looking hurt and bewildered. Searching the pallid face, Garthan found the gray eyes clear of alien shadow; relief that was almost too keen lanced through him and left him shaken.

Isolated on the white expanse of the clearing, they steadied each other while their racing hearts slowed and the sweat on their faces turned to rime. The cold began to penetrate Haston's clothing, and he looked around as if he had just realized where they stood.

"Please." His voice faltered, and he shuddered. "I don't have my cloak . . . Let's go inside." He turned back toward the bothy, but Garthan's hard hand shackled his wrist.

"No." Garthan was grim. "We'll not spend another night within those walls."

"But—we'll freeze outside. Where will we stay? What are you doing?"

"You'll see." Garthan was wrapping his own cloak about Haston. "Stay here," Garthan admonished, and plunged back to enter the bothy. He emerged in moments with Haston's cloak and their bedding heaped in his arms. He jerked his head at the rough shed beside the bothy.

"Tell the horses to move over," he said. "We're coming to spend the night." Looking up toward the sky he added, "See— the snow's stopped. Tomorrow we can be gone from here."

Haston clutched Garthan's cloak tighter about him as they trudged back toward the shed. He dug his hands in the pockets for warmth and stubbed his fingertips on a small hard wad in one of them. He snatched it out, sure what it was even before he looked. With shaking fingers he unfolded the scrap of vellum, almost afraid of what might be written there.

"Where did you find this?" he demanded.

"What? That? Up the chimney, stuck between two stones. Couldn't make any sense of it. Meant to show it to you but I forgot. What's it say?"

Silently Haston read the brief passage:

. . . he will help me. I lay the hides out for cutting. Rahk looks and says, one is mine, I know it by the scars on the head. Remember, when I skin it I show it to you. I say, it is so, but how does it get in my cache. He says, who should know but you. He had made it look like *I* am thief. Now I hate him. But I do not say this. Tonight when he thinks I sleep, I watch to catch him. Again he sees me write. What if he somehow learns my plan. Somehow I hide this

"Well, what is it?" Garthan repeated.

Haston let the wind snatch the fragment of vellum away from his chilled fingers and watched it vanish in the snow.

"Nothing," he murmured, "just—the end of an old story."

Here, in a very small space, are two people turning around each other with the inexorable necessity of an orrery.

THE COTTAGE IN WINTER

BY MCNEVIN HAYES

The frame had warped around the heavy glass of the skylight, and though it didn't leak, it groaned and chirped. Rain slapped the walls and roof; wind battered the trees.

Gene sat in the oak chair, looking out the bay window, his feet on the sill. Neither he nor his brother had shaved since their arrival. Gene's face was soft and sparsely bearded; Kevin was younger by two years, but his beard was heavier and his face harder. Kevin knelt at the fireplace, stacking wood on the grate.

"Carol is pregnant."

"What?" Gene said.

"Carol is pregnant." His voice was an almost inaudible sing-song.

"Are you sure?"

"Yeah. We're sure. She wouldn't lie about it. Betty used to tell me she was pregnant to see how I'd react." He rolled a sheet of newspaper and stuffed it under the grate.

"I remember." Gene turned the chair and resettled in it, facing him. Kevin, for Kevin, looked pale. "Carol wouldn't do that. But I thought you were being careful."

Kevin shrugged listlessly. "So did I. I thought at first it had to be by someone else. We made love only once without a rubber, and I made sure not to come in her. But the doctor told us that men lubricate with a little bit of sperm. I hadn't known that. They never told us in sex education. Someone ought to sue the schools. I was always careful." He wiped greasy ash on his pants leg.

"What do you think you'll do?"

"I don't know yet. Neither does she. But I'm not going to let her down, and I'm not going to let myself down. I'm not going to run away."

"That's why you wanted to come up here?"

Kevin nodded. "I have to sort things out."

"So you don't suspect anyone else as father?" Gene asked.

"Not unless it's you," Kevin said. He lit a match.

"Kevin, that's bullshit."

Kevin shrugged and watched flames crawl along the edges of the paper.

"We only kissed good-night. Christ, Kevin, we were back early enough. How long have you been mad about that? You said you weren't then. We talked; that was it. We like one another. She took me to a movie because I was broke and she wanted to talk."

Kevin shrugged again. "I guess I don't think you fucked. I'm not mad; don't get excited." He stood. "I was just being bitter. I'm sorry. But I still think you shouldn't have taken her out."

"She took me out."

"You could have said no." He pulled the nunchucks from between the couch cushions.

"It's not like I was 'making time' with her. She's an old friend of the family's."

"This has nothing to do with my problem. I want to drop the subject. It's funny to me that you get mad when I don't react the way you expect me to." He tucked the nunchucks under his arm, cradling them, and stared hard at the fire. Kevin had been attending a dojo for almost a year. Gene knew that his brother was good; he had seen Kevin study the philosophy of the art as well as his katas, and knew karate brought Kevin self-esteem.

There was nothing Gene could say. Why had Kevin asked him along? For the gas money? He turned to the window. Foam crested the rising gray swells, and the sky was darkening. The 'chucks whistled in front of the fire. Gene realized his hand was in a fist. He relaxed it and tried to relax his neck.

After a while he said, "We'd better do something about the boat."

Kevin was silent until Gene thought he hadn't heard, then said, "I tied it well."

"That doesn't matter. There isn't a cover on it. It may be half full by now."

"The rain will give it a good cleaning."

"I don't think you understand; it's become a northeaster. See?" He pointed at the wind vane one of the neighbors had posted on the beach.

Kevin spun the nunchucks over and under his shoulders, staring down into the couch. Then he let them clatter there. He looked out the window. Gene had crossed the room; he lifted their coats from the rack by the door. He tossed Kevin's and Kevin snapped it from the air, quickly, in the moment that it hovered. Gene pulled on his watch cap and they went out.

They rounded the bushes at the corner; Gene's eyes teared in the wind.

Kevin said, "I think we're wasting our time." His face was expressionless.

"Well, I think it's time you learned to be careful," Gene said. Kevin slapped him across the top of the head; Gene's cap fell and he stumbled into a bush. Rain cascaded from the needles and down his leg. He jumped back, furious.

Kevin glowered into his eyes with his jaw jutted forward. He was poised to block, punch, or kick. Seeing Gene was not ready to fight, he skipped back a half step and danced lightly, his fists floating. Gene bent very slowly and retrieved his cap. He stuffed it in his coat pocket, then straightened.

"I wish you could see what an asshole you've become," Gene said. It was the only sort of blow he knew he could get through.

Kevin shoved him in the chest. Gene's feet slid; he twisted as he fell; his palm, then his elbow, hit. Mud splashed his side; pain darted from his elbow to his shoulder. He had jerked his knees high and he rested on his heels and one arm with his stomach in the air. Kevin turned impassively and went back the way they'd come. His shoulders were stiff, his head more erect than with pride.

Gene shifted his weight onto his feet, pushing gingerly off his sore arm. He gasped and continued to crouch. Grass dipped around him in the rain. He stood, full of hate, and opened his coat and shirt. He massaged his arm on the way to the beach. The drops that hit him through the leaves were large, slow and cold. When he was halfway down the slope the drops became quick and sharp. He shivered and buttoned his shirt. His hair whipped about in the wind, hurting his scalp.

The boat was an old wooden rowboat, painted green, with a twelve-horse outboard. Waves broke across the stern. The rope from the prow to the tree, slack when they'd left it, was taut.

He stuffed an inflated roller under the bow. Then he took hold of the rope and threw his weight down and back. His heels drove into the wet sand and the boat edged forward; a wave hit it and carried it back. He tried again, and again it dragged back. His shoulder ached.

He went into the lake to his knees. The high surf was warmer than the air. Bracing himself, he tipped the boat onto one side. Even while some of the water poured out, waves licked around the engine and sloshed into the hull. He let the boat fall upright. He wanted to scream. He wanted to smash the boat to splinters.

He looked up and saw Kevin waiting at the rope.

Face to face, they pulled the boat high enough to drain. Kevin yanked with violent surges that did most of the work until the boat fell forward, crookedly, off the roller. After draining it, they hauled it up the slope and past the tree. Kevin tied the tarp down while Gene returned the roller to the shed. Behind them, the lake thundered onto the shore.

"Thanks," Gene said guardedly. Kevin nodded. Gene wished either of them could have meant it; then it would not have had to be said. Kevin led the way back to the house; his broad back was like a shield.

Gene was abruptly shocked by the pain locked in his brother's shoulders. How had Kevin's pain and fear gotten so vast that he could not be reached? How had this been done to him? Gene wanted to rewrite his brother's history, rearrange his life, his entire world. He did not want to wait out the rain in a small space with this monster.

I now offer you one of the shortest (and best) deal-with-the-devil stories I have ever read.

LOADED DICE

BY RENA LEITH

The little man in the red suit awkwardly approached the group of children. He kept hitching up his tights and tripping over his tail. It had not been a good week.

"Damned regulations," he muttered.

The little girl watched him. When he was ten feet away, she asked, "You going to a party, mister?"

He smiled blandly, moved closer and squatted in the dust of the playground next to her. "Do you know who I am?"

"No."

"I mean, if I tell you that my suit is real, then do you know who I am?"

"Yup." She picked up her jacks.

"Who?"

She looked at him again. "The devil."

He exhaled. "Good. What do devils do?"

"Bad things."

"Do you know what a soul is?"

"Uh-huh."

He sighed. She idly bounced her jack ball.

"I want your soul."

"Why?"

"Because that's my job."

"Why?"

"Because I'm a devil."

"Why?"

He wiped his face. "What are you doing?"

"Playing jacks."

"Can I play with you?"

She stared at him, eyes narrowed. "Well . . ."

"Tell you what. One game. If I lose, I'll give you this new ball and leave. If I win, you give me your soul."

She shrugged. "Sure."

He settled down in the dirt next to her. "Okay. How do you play?"

"You have to bounce the ball and pick up the jacks."

"How many do you have to pick up?"

"How old are you?"

"One hundred and three."

"That many."

"But you don't have that many jacks."

"I win." She picked up her jacks, her old ball and the new one. She looked up and pointed behind him. "I hope your daddy doesn't spank you."

He decided not to look.

"Bye-bye."

*Here was the graveyard, and here were the Baums, the
Davidsons, the Hirsches—but where were the Sinsheimers?
Had the world grown so small that there was no room left for
the dead?*

VINES

BY LOIS WICKSTROM

Sarah didn't want to go to Germany. One of the reasons she had
taken her husband's name when they married was to get rid of
her father's Germanic one. Sarah was descended from Jews who
had emigrated from Germany before World War I. But they had
carried with them a Germanic name that would always pull them
back.

Sarah's parents were divorced. Her mother had been traded in
for a younger, blonder model with bigger breasts, and that
model, too, had been traded in, each trade separating her more
from her father. And she had transferred some of the insecurity
she felt with her father to her husband, fearing that he might
leave her, the way her father had left her mother: without warning.

But now she was going to Germany—well, her husband was
going to Germany, and she was coming with, which of course
meant she would have free time, which of course meant she could
trace down some family roots.

Roots was the wrong word. Vines, she called them. Her family
had never dug into the soil. They could barely crawl along the
surface before somebody scraped them off. But in Germany there
would be permanent gravestones of buried ancestors. So it wasn't
too much of a surprise when she received a phone call from her
mother.

Despite the divorce, her mother was still interested in the Sinsheimer family mystery. "And Sinsheim is so close to Heidelberg, where your husband's meeting is."

"But why," Sarah asked, "would I want to go to a town that was mean to my ancestors?" The story that had been passed down was that the family used to be named Baum, but sometime around 1700, when it came time to register for taxes, the judge who did the registering was also named Baum, and he would not allow a Jewish family to register with his surname. Therefore, Sarah's ancestors had taken the name of the town. At the time this wasn't a big issue. After all, in the 1700s last names were a pretty new thing, and traditions weren't yet attached to them.

"It can't have been so bad," her mother insisted. "They must have been proud of the town to want to take its name."

Or to have the last laugh, thought Sarah. "Okay, I'll go, but I won't promise to find anything."

Sarah packed her camera, which was a big old twin-lens reflex —the kind that is heavy and a nuisance and reliable. And she packed six rolls of film: color, black-and-white, and color slide. She also packed a flash attachment and spare batteries. All these she put into her backpack, which would instantly mark her as an American.

And she packed her usual excess of clothing: skirts (even though she always wore pants), stockings (even though she preferred socks), and extra underwear (because you've always got to have clean underwear). Reuben, her husband, packed his own bags, including the papers for the meeting. Together they packed a sack of vegetables to eat on the plane. Kosher meals always came with a piece of paper apologizing for the lack of a salad. The paper claimed that this was due to the necessities of kosher preparation, but Sarah didn't know of any kosher regulations that said you couldn't have a salad on an airplane.

The airplane ride was uneventful. All announcements were in both English and German. The airplane seemed to be a study in overpopulation. Screaming babies, smoke wafting in from the smokers' section, toddlers kicking the seats of the passengers in front of them, skimpy meals. Sarah was glad they had ordered kosher, but it felt odd getting a larger meal *because* she was Jewish. She had a sudden image of Germany, as crowded as the airplane, and wondered where an overcrowded country would put its thousands of years of graveyards.

And as if to feed her worst fears, after nine hours of flight, the announcer said, "The airport at Frankfurt is closed in. We will circle for an hour." Sarah felt sick to her stomach.

Around and around went the plane, and Sarah heard a voice that she knew had not been broadcast over the public address system, a voice like the one she had heard at the dinner table before her parents' divorce—an unspoken voice of warning. This time it said, "There isn't enough fuel." She thought about telling Reuben, but what good would it do? Then two of them would know that their plane could not make it. Shortly before the hour was up, the announcer claimed their attention again. "Ladies and gentlemen, we will be diverted to Cologne for refueling." Someone up front must have heard the warning, too, or at least read the gauges, thought Sarah. And she was again reminded that her family had left Germany *before* World War I. Had they heard the voices? Where had they gained the courage to act on these voices? She had tried sometimes to warn people, but nobody had believed her.

Their airplane landed in Cologne.

"Let's get out," said Sarah. "If we catch a train from here, we'll get to Heidelberg faster than if we wait and fly back to Frankfurt."

"What excuse can we give them?" asked Reuben.

"Tell them I'm sick. I don't care. I'm tired of being crowded and breathing stale air and being in an airplane."

Again the announcement: "We have obtained landing clearance. We are returning to Frankfurt." Sarah swallowed and tried to act both brave and enthusiastic, the way she would have when she was eight.

"See?" Reuben said. "A train wouldn't have been this fast."

"Let's wait and see."

When they reached Frankfurt, the plane began to circle again, and Sarah tried to pretend she was on a ride at an amusement park. Some people paid good money to go in circles. She had paid her money to go in a straight line. Somehow the attendants had simply put her on the wrong ride. She remembered being jealous of people who got stuck on the top of the Ferris wheel. She tried to tell herself that she was getting an extra turn.

"We are in a holding pattern, awaiting our turn for entry," came the voice on the loudspeaker. "We can expect to land in about an hour and a half."

"Think they'll give us some extra food?" asked Reuben.

"Are you kidding?"

"They didn't even apologize." Reuben frowned.

"Did they apologize for either of the World Wars?"

Heidelberg was filled with old architecture. Buildings appeared to be held up by carved men. Angular rooms stuck out over narrow streets. Posters of naked women, or photographs or statues of naked men, advertised assorted products. One photo showed a teenage girl squeezing a pimple. And a McDonald's nestled into an ornate seventeenth-century building.

Overlooking the city was the castle. Little doorways carved into bigger doors, all overhung with fearsome spikes that Sarah hoped had rusted into place. Statues of knights, carvings of lions in various stages of roaring. Cobbled streets and walks, fresh-fruit stands, sweetshops—it looked like the original model for Berkeley, California, and even had a university renowned for activist students. It seemed that everyone was named Bitteh; the guidebook said the word was pronounced "bitter" and meant "please." Bitteh, would you give me this? Bitteh, would you kindly do that? And all the faces seemed repressed. "Life is bitter," quipped Sarah. No one let her speak guidebook German; they all had to try out their American on her.

Sarah bought fresh fruit and vegetables at the markets. Something about the nature of restaurant preparation prevented the hotel management from serving them salads. Sarah didn't know of anything in kosher law that prevented her from eating vegetables in her hotel room. Or, for that matter, yogurt and chocolate bars. All the Sinsheimers had a craving for chocolate—bittersweet chocolate, to be precise.

Sarah took long walks and bought gifts for relatives—cut crystal, candelabra, and of course chocolate bars. But she could not postpone forever the trip to Sinsheim. It was only a half-hour train ride, and the trains ran on time. Her mother had told her Sinsheim was a walled city, which it was not. She had expected to find someone named Sinsheimer in the phone book, which she did not. And she expected to find a city historical museum, which existed but was closed, and the locals told her it was mainly full of old bicycles anyway.

It took Sarah only a few minutes in the town to know why her ancestors had left: it was boring. Nothing new had been built here in centuries. It was a town for short people, and Sarah was short. Walks down alleyways revealed doors through which an ordinary American would need to stoop. Overhanging roofs made Reuben, who was over five feet tall, bow his head. And residents looked suspiciously at a pair of Americans (Sarah was wearing her backpack) walking in the private parts of their town. Sarah was amazed that her relatives had lived here at all.

In the central shopping area there was a town map, obviously provided by some tourist bureau, even though the entirety of Sinsheim could be walked in half an hour. Reuben loved maps. Sarah immediately found the graveyards—one for Jews, the other for Christians, but both marked with crosses. Then she waited patiently for Reuben to have his map-staring ritual. She wanted to say, "We're here, and the gravestones are there—let's walk," but they would probably never return to Sinsheim, and this was the sort of highly detailed map that Reuben dearly loved, so she walked along the storefronts, staring at grouchy mannequins with messy hair, and when that grew boring she tried to pick out patterns in the cobbles of the street. She had found a series of intersecting arches when Reuben said, "Let's go."

The Jewish graveyard was along a little-used road at the end of town, and the entry gate was locked. Unkempt bushes surrounded it, yet there was no sense of awe or foreboding in this graveyard. The sky was clear above, the graveyard was simply a green field with stones in it, an innocent pastoral setting. Sarah and Reuben squeezed their way between branches, took separate rows, and systematically began their hunt for Sinsheimers.

"Here's a Baum, and a Davidson, and an Oppenheimer," called Sarah.

"And here are some more Baums and a Rosenheimer and a Hirsh," said Reuben.

"What are Baums doing here if they got their name changed?" she asked.

"Maybe there's something wrong with your family's story."

"Or maybe that mean old judge's family repented and converted," said Sarah. "Let's keep looking."

Farther from the roadway, the graveyard was even more unkempt. Gravestones were completely overgrown with vines. Branches of trees occluded some of the passageways. A few family stones had blank spots, as if the family had left town before its members could finish dying. But what became even more and more unnerving was the dates on the stones: all of them between 1900 and 1930.

"But of course, Sinsheim is not the sort of town anyone would go back to after a war. Anyplace would be better." Sarah felt an urge to yank the vines off the gravestones. Then she felt an even stronger pull to photograph the gravestones as they were. It did not matter if they hid her ancestors. Those vines symbolized her ancestors far better than a name on a stone. And they symbolized Germany's attitude toward Jews, and no, she was making too much of it—but it would be a good photograph to show the relatives back home.

"What do they do? Recycle graves?" she asked.

"Sure looks like it. See, in that corner, there are some vacant spaces."

"And some kicked-over gravestones."

"There's only room for about forty years of stones."

"It's like an overpopulation story, about a world where there isn't even room for the dead."

"Then what's the point of being buried at all?"

"What's the point of being buried anyway?"

They had had that discussion before.

Sarah systematically photographed all the gravestones that said "Baum," and Reuben lifted the toppled stones, revealing some more Baum children. Sarah photographed them, too. "There is definitely something wrong with that story," she said. "That name change was supposed to have happened two centuries before these gravestones were carved. Let's go check out the other half of the story; let's see if there are any Baums in the Christian graveyard."

"You want to go to a Christian graveyard?"

Sarah replaced her camera in her backpack, and they again squeezed between the bushes and out onto the weedy road. A child walked a dog past them and stared as if to say, "You don't look Jewish."

A few blocks away was the Christian graveyard, with its wrought-iron gates wide open and fresh flowers growing on graves. Paved walkways led along rows of polished gravestones, and people dressed in fine clothes chatted beside statues or in front of bouquets. Sarah and Reuben held hands and walked briskly down the rows. They saw no Baums, no Sinsheimers, and no gravestones dated earlier than 1940.

And Sarah had a sudden horrible thought that the Germans were going to dig up the Jewish graveyard so their own people could stay buried longer. She told Reuben what she was thinking.

"No one can deny that they've had their forty years in the ground. You couldn't call it discrimination," he said.

"But, if they do, ours may be the last generation able to solve the mystery of the Sinsheimers, and we're going home in a week."

Sarah could see that a country that made a habit of starting world wars would want to wipe out history. Digging up gravestones, erasing ancestors, changing names—it all fitted the pattern. When the graveyard was recycled, it was time for another war.

Sarah recalled the story of a cousin who had been in Sinsheim with the American military. The cousin had gotten drunk and had been arrested, but when he presented his identification, he had said, *"Ich bin ein Sinsheimer,"* and instead of putting him in jail, the mayor had treated him to a fancy dinner. And she wondered if forgetting history made them kinder on a personal level, along with being crueler on a world level.

Reuben led her out of the graveyard, back into town. They stopped at a sweetshop for slices of chocolate cake. The faces around them were the same intelligent repressed faces they had seen before the graveyard. Now Sarah knew how dangerous they could be. "Come on," she said to Reuben, "let's get out of here."

"Is there time to finish my cake?" he asked.

The next morning, Sarah arrayed the contents of her backpack on one side of the bed while Reuben checked over his briefcase on the other. "May I have the guidebook today?" she asked.

"Sure," said Reuben, "if I can have the dictionary."

Trees were fighting outside their window as a gusty rain grayed the city.

"Are you going to be safe out in that stuff?" he asked.

"I won't melt. Besides, bad weather is supposed to discourage criminals more than decent folks."

"Still, you ought to have an umbrella."

"I'll borrow one at the door."

Reuben snapped his briefcase shut. "You're sure you know where you're going?"

Reuben always looked so hopeful when he asked this question that she hated to shatter his confidence once again. Still, she was very good at getting lost, and could take an hour to go half a mile by making every conceivable wrong turn. So she asked, "When I get to the light, do I go left or right to the train station?"

He said, "You turn right and go about six blocks. Then you cross the street and get in the *fahrkarten* line."

Sarah smiled. "Thanks."

Once she was on the train, she stored the borrowed green-and-yellow umbrella in an overhead rack where it could drip on the back of the seat, against the wall. She was alone in the no-smoking cubicle, and she wondered if regular train riders brought towels for their umbrellas to drip on.

Once she was settled, she allowed her gaze to wander out the window. There were orderly gardens heavy with fruit. The land looked cared for. Sarah had very mixed feelings about how to react. On the one hand, Germans had declared war on her people. On the other, her ancestors had lived here. To reject this country totally was to reject part of herself that she didn't even know. If she were to believe the family stories, her ancestors had lived respected lives here for several centuries. Since they had stayed, there must have been something good here. Why else were all the Jews here for Hitler's men to kill? It must have been something very good indeed. Or else they didn't hear the voices, or didn't act. Would she have the courage to break the window and jump out of the train if a voice told her it was going to slip off the tracks? The train pulled into Sinsheim.

Gripping her umbrella handle tightly, Sarah felt she had the right to be here. Her ancestors had walked these cobbled streets, traversed these narrow alleys. German was one language she hadn't taken in school, and this lack of knowledge suddenly seemed like a wall; if she could break through it, she could grasp the vine that tied her to the mystery, to her ancestors, to herself.

She did not need to know German to recognize the broad heavy steps of the city hall. She tried to feel those marble slabs through the bottoms of her shoes, imagining how they must have felt to her unsuspecting ancestors who had climbed them with one name and left with another.

The clerk looked like her equivalent in America, except perhaps more grown up. This woman who possibly held the key to Sarah's mystery had been accepted by her elders, her culture—she belonged. Sarah folded her umbrella and placed it in the corner to drip with the others. Surely in this town it would not be stolen.

"Sprecken zee English?" she asked hopefully.

"A little."

Since Sarah no longer trusted the family story, and because unaccountably she desired this stranger's respect, she simply said, "My maiden name is Sinsheimer. I think I may have had ancestors in this town. Do you have any old tax records here that I could look at?"

"One moment," said the clerk, and left the room.

Was my speech too long? she wondered. Is the clerk looking for someone who can translate for us? Time passed. The puddle by the umbrellas grew, and Sarah wondered if the clerk was summoning the mayor to take her to lunch. How would she explain her food requirements to the mayor? She began to pace and wonder if they were going to arrest her for having broken an unknown taboo. Perhaps, after her cousin's escapade, someone had already checked the records and knew that the Sinsheimers were Jewish. Maybe they were simply waiting for her to go away so they could avoid a scene.

There were clickings and clumpings on the floor, and the clerk returned with a slim elderly gentleman who looked as if he had memorized hundreds of years of certificates for taxes, weddings, births, deaths, and real estate transactions.

"He does not speak English," said the clerk. "He says 'Sinsheimer' is a Jewish name."

Sarah felt sweat break out, even on her stomach. If her clothes had been elastic, they would have slid right off. "What else can he tell me?" she asked. In the silence of the room, she could feel the clerk thinking, "Is she Jewish?"

"They left town nearly a century ago. They were very much like you, I'm told. A look about the eyes like they had never grown up. This isn't a town for dreamers, so they left."

"But," asked Sarah, wondering if there was a lighted billboard on her forehead displaying her emotions in flux, "can you tell me how they got the name?"

"They probably chose it," said the clerk. "Jews are always changing their names." Suddenly she shut her mouth, as if remembering that this was not a safe topic.

"Yes," said Sarah, "but do you know why they did it? What it used to be? Jews always say what their names are changed from for several generations at least."

The clerk and the elderly gentleman conferred in German for a while, and then the clerk left Sarah and the old man alone staring at each other.

Before the tension became intolerable, the clerk returned with an older, stouter woman and said, inclining her head toward Sarah, "Her maiden name was Sinsheimer. Go with them to the cellar and translate for them, please." The clerk opened a swinging door in the counter and motioned Sarah to pass through.

Sarah thought, they could kill me down there and nobody would ever find me. Look, she chided herself, I came here to solve a mystery. The only way out is through. Then she thought: now I sound like a religious martyr. My life for a document. How did I get myself into this situation?

The elderly gentleman was holding the door for her. She swallowed, took a deep breath, and walked into the passageway. They went down dimly lit stairs, the lady first, then Sarah and finally the gentleman, two steps behind.

The steps turned at a landing, becoming even more dim. Sarah's heart raced. When they reached the base of the stairs, the lady pulled a cord and a bulb lit up. Then she whirled around, hands on hips. Her eyes seemed to glow. Sarah stepped back in terror, losing her balance against the stairs. The gentleman caught her by the shoulders and held her firmly. Now they've got me, she thought. Should I try to run away, or should I relax and hope they don't hurt me too much? The lady said something in German. The gentleman let go of Sarah and pointed to his left.

"I stumbled," said Sarah.

"Are you hurt?" asked the lady.

"I don't think so," said Sarah, and thought—at least not yet.

"Then come."

To the left was a room like a library filled with rows of floor-to-ceiling bookshelves. But here all the books were alike, gray-green, fat, and labeled by hand with the year and alphabetical symbols. The books looked as if they might have been a nice shade of green once but had faded. Sarah had a hard time picturing sunlight coming down those stairs into this windowless cellar, and the bare incandescent bulbs overhead couldn't bleach a blonde's hair. Perhaps these books had been in a windowed room once where young people happily registered their homes, recorded the births of their children and thought the government was a nuisance to make them record the daily details of their lives. If it weren't for nosy governments, she thought, I'd never be able to trace my ancestors.

The elderly Germans were still conversing. Sarah stood gazing at the rows upon rows of records that held information that was no longer of use to the state, but only to searchers like herself. It was a wonder they didn't charge admission. Sarah had thought of records as being typewritten forms, but this was like a museum where they kept handwritten things like orders to hang witches.

"Dear," asked the lady, "is there any memory in your family of the name being something else?"

Fear hit Sarah's stomach like an arrow severing her guts. Should I lie? she asked herself. And then she thought, if they are going to hurt me, I guess they will, and if they are going to help me, I may as well help all of us and shorten the hunt if I can. "Some say it used to be Baum."

"Oh, there used to be Baums around here fifty or sixty years ago. I went to school with Gerta Baum. That was an old family; they had long roots in this town, but they moved away—I think to Frankfurt. Do you think you might be related to them? I can probably arrange for you to meet them. Gerta used to talk about how her family was supposed to be the only true Baum family in town. That there had been another one but her ancestors made them—I'll bet that's you! And after all these years, you're here and they aren't."

"But there are Baums in the Jewish graveyard," blurted Sarah.

"Oh, you've been there already."

Sarah couldn't read the woman's face.

"I looked at both graveyards yesterday," she said, hoping the lady wouldn't know that the Jewish graveyard was locked.

The old man spoke again, his words incomprehensible. He must feel left out, thought Sarah. I wish we could look at the books.

The woman spoke in German, yet looked at Sarah as she

might look at an item for sale. Sarah felt herself flinch and willed her clothes to become armor.

"You don't want to know about those Baums," the lady said, in the sort of voice that fifth-grade teachers use to close discussions of sexy pictures.

Sarah's immediate thought was, why not? But then she thought, they probably aren't my relatives. This isn't my country. I don't have time to make trouble just for the fun of it. In her most obedient-sounding voice, she said, "May I see the records of the old Baum family?"

"You'll have to forgive us. Sinsheim was slow about setting up a system of records. Sinsheim has always been a small town. Who needs records if you already know everything about everybody? But then around seventeen hundred the duke's ministers made us have paper records. That is probably when the name change occurred."

Sarah started to feel like a parrot. "Could I see the books, please?" She wondered if these old folks were stalling for some sinister reason. The two of them could subdue her. They wouldn't need reinforcements.

More German conversations, with an occasional "zee" that Sarah knew meant "you" and was spelled "Sie." She couldn't help picturing the cartoon Italian chef talking about "zee macaroni," and smiled in spite of herself.

The old gentleman walked to the end of the farthest aisle, his steps going click, scuff on the worn cement floor. He bent, and Sarah expected him to creak, but he did not. His fingers rested gently on one grayed volume, moved to another as if he had to touch a book to be able to read its spine. Finally he pulled one out, stood and returned. He gave it to the lady. She turned the book open at the middle and flipped pages over in clumps, working her way to the back. With each plop of paper on paper, Sarah's heart raced, and her fingers stretched, readying themselves to hold the book, feel the pages, touch the history.

Finally the lady stopped and said crisply, "Here, this is what you came to see." It was followed by a silent "Be gone."

The unspoken voice said, "It will be safe here."

Old paper has a smell of its own. It isn't dusty or musty the way poets describe it. Before her fingertips touched the book, Sarah felt engulfed in it. She grasped the book with both hands and sat down on the cold cracked floor. Her thighs cringed as she made her legs bend campfire-style to support the book. She ran her fingers along the edges of the pages and checked her fingertips for paper cuts. Then she remembered that only cheap paper is sharp-edged, and cheap paper couldn't have lasted nearly three hundred years. That scene with Weener and the time traveler where he smashed the books only applied to modern paperbacks. And this book was as old as George Washington.

The German script looked almost alien, but then her mind adjusted, just as her eyes had become accustomed to the pale bulbs dangling from the ceiling. There before her was the slanty signature of Simon Sinsheimer. "Sinsheimer" was written in the space above the word Baum. The Baum signature had one clean line drawn lightly through the middle, as if Simon had wanted everyone to know what his name used to be. The name "Sinsheimer" looked awkward, the way Reuben's name had looked when she first started using it as her own. The handwriting was pointy and slanted markedly to the right, like her own. The *m* in Simon was made with two close rounded humps, a V-shaped gap and a third lower pointy bump. There was a long pen line after the final *n* in Simon as if he'd been reluctant to lift his hand from the form. Was this when the argument had begun about the name?

Sarah wanted to turn the pages and see if there were any other changed names. She looked up at the Germans. They looked impatient. Still, this was her trip, her history . . .

"Could I see the other books, so I may see what year they left town?"

More talking in German.

"We close soon. We will leave you down here to look. All the old books are here," said the woman. Then she went upstairs, and the man walked slowly to another part of the basement. Sarah thought, what if they close me in here? And then she thought, well, if they do, they will open up tomorrow . . . But how could I go to sleep without my head on Reuben's shoulder? She stood up, her legs tingling with the cold from the floor, and walked to the shelf from which her book had been taken. She pulled out the next book and turned to the place where Simon's name ought to have been. It wasn't there. She looked through the entire book, page by page, wondering if it had been misfiled. But she couldn't find it. She had a momentary twinge of feeling incompetent. If only the old gentleman or the lady had opened the book, it would have been there, but no, she had to be the one, and now it was gone. She checked the next several books for Simon Baum and Simon Sinsheimer, but neither was listed.

One piece of paper with Simon's signature. That was it—her roots; ground up and turned into paper, written on by one dead ancestor. Where had he gone? What had he done in his life? He hadn't even left a train-ticket stub in this book so she could follow him, not even a letter of protest, or the name of the synagogue where he had gone to have it out with God over this indignity. This was a dead end. Just as dead as the unrelated Baums in the graveyard with vines crawling all over them.

Was this what she would tell her mother? That she, who couldn't always find something that she had placed on her own desk, had found proof of an old family story? Was this supposed to solve something? Did this make Germany a worthwhile country, because it held this one piece of paper?

She had received more pleasure from the architecture, or even the chocolate bars. If the story had turned out to be wrong or undocumentable, what would that have meant? But the record was here. The people of this country destroyed graveyards and kept tax forms. They killed people, even destroyed their names, but kept their signatures.

She remembered the voice telling her, "It will be safe here." And she thought, why, buried underground in an obscure city like this one, this record will probably survive the coming world war. There will be some Sinsheimers who survive it too, and they will come here. I will leave them something that may help their search. She took a piece of stationery from her backpack and wrote on it. "I was here in 1982. I live in America. It wouldn't do any good for me to write my address because we move so often. I am still Jewish, just like Simon, and I will raise my children that way too. We are not related to the Baums in the graveyard, according to the clerk who helped me find this book. It feels funny communicating with you this way, but I want you to know that I do hear the voices, and I know they do not lie. And I think our family will hang on." She signed it "Sarah Sinsheimer." The "Sinsheimer" looked awkward, since she had not written it in years. She placed it next to Simon's page in the book.

You do want the best for your unborn child, don't you? All right, suppose you could have the best—intelligence, talent, beauty, everything. How much would you pay?

THIRD PRIZE

PURSUIT OF EXCELLENCE

BY RENA YOUNT

It was a late summer afternoon, and the city of Washington lay quiet in a warm light rain. A minibus hissed over wet pavement, gliding driverless through the traffic loop at Calvert Street, past the towers and multilevel malls, the pedwalks where shoppers rode with their bright umbrellas. Evelyn Barr sat by a bus window: a slender woman in her thirties, with wide cheekbones and a pointed chin.

She was tired. She worked days as a chemist and most evenings as a waitress. She would just have time, today, to stop by home and make sure everything was all right before heading on to her second job. But she watched the rain-blurred mosaic of the passing city with an almost proprietary sense of satisfaction. It was a smoother, cleaner, brighter city than it had been when she moved into it fifteen years before. Make better people, she thought, and they will put the rest of the world in order.

My daughter will be one of them, she thought, the familiar tingle of anticipation coming warm and strong. The time was getting close at last.

As she let herself into her apartment, she called, "Randy?"

"In here, Mom," her nine-year-old answered. She went into his room to give him a kiss. His terminal was on and covered with graphs. "Homework?" she asked.

"Yeah. I want to get done before Dad gets home so he can help me with my model satellite."

"Good thinking," she said. She ruffled his hair. It was dark, like hers, but curly and unruly, while hers was straight and fine. He had her brown eyes, and her dimples when he smiled.

"Did you lay out your clothes to wash?" she asked.

"Uh-huh. Then I put them in the washer with the other stuff. Then I washed them. It seemed like a good idea. They're in the dryer now."

"Wonderful!" she said. "Now I'll have time for a cup of coffee before I go."

He looked up at her sideways. "Can I have some too?"

"Coffee? Now, you know that's not for children. It'd keep you awake all night."

"Just a little? I did the laundry."

"Well—just a little. With milk."

She hung up her raincoat and went into the kitchen to check the freezer. She and her husband Michael cooked on the weekends and froze portions for dinner during the week. Usually Michael would be home on nights when she worked, but sometimes his own job as production manager for a small publisher kept him late. Randy had had to mature more quickly than a lot of kids; they counted on him to take care of himself when he had to, and to help with work around the apartment.

"What would you like for dinner?" she called to him. "Chicken casserole or nut loaf?"

"Which one did I cut up the mushrooms for?" he asked.

"Nut loaf," she said.

"I want that one."

"Fine," she said, smiling. She began making a salad. The kitchen was small, like all the rooms in their apartment; housing was expensive. But it was neat and well organized, an easy place to work. She moved quickly from sink to counter, rinsing and chopping lettuce and green peppers. Randy called from his room. "Guess what I got for homework."

She set one oven compartment on Thaw/Cook and started the timer. "What?" she asked.

"I get to be president this week."

"Of the class?"

"No, silly. Of Skolania. That's the country our class gets to be, for simulation. Come and look."

"Just a minute." She put Michael's dinner in another compartment and set the controls. As she went into Randy's room she said, "Now, your dinner will be ready in half an hour, so listen for the bell. And don't forget to start Dad's at eight, because he'll be home at eight-thirty and he'll be hungry. It's all set—just push 'Start.' "

"Look at this," Randy said.

"And there's salad in the refrigerator. Are you listening?"

"Sure. Eight o'clock. In the refrigerator. I'll remember. Look here."

He was standing before his terminal. There was a stool for him to sit on, but he rarely used it. He preferred to bounce from foot to foot, jiggling, his slim body full of energy.

"Okay," she said, perching on the stool. "I'm looking."

"See, for this project we have five variables. There's population —that's how many people you have. And there's money for agriculture—that's how much you spend for seeds and tractors and stuff. Then there's money for defense, to buy planes and everything, and workers for agriculture, and workers for defense. And if you're president you have to mess around with all of those so they come out right. Only Kenny Blake was president last week, and boy, did he leave everything in a mess."

Evelyn smiled. Even kids blamed the previous administration.

"See, if you put more money in for agriculture, you get more soybeans." He moved a control, and little rows of green soybean plants ran up one side of the screen. "For a while. But then you don't get any more unless you put more *workers* in too. To use all the tractors and junk. But that means less workers for defense." Sure enough, little blue figures with rifles were disappearing from the DEFENSE graph as he turned a knob. "And Botania, that's the other fourth-grade class, they might start a war. I mean, maybe they won't, but they might. Mary Sue's in that class, and she *loves* to start wars. But, see, if you don't get enough soybeans then people will starve. Only, you know what?"

"What?" she asked.

He leaned close to the stool and whispered to her. A secret. "I *hate* soybeans."

Suddenly he was bouncing up and down, twirling knobs, yelling, "Yukh! Die, soybeans! Down with soybeans!" Evelyn laughed. Little green plants blipped off the screen by the dozen, the population chart began to glow a warning red, and then a yellow neon flashing began: FAMINE. FAMINE.

Randy giggled, looking at her sideways. "I wouldn't *really* do that," he explained.

"I'm sure you wouldn't."

"I just like to hear what the vice-president's going to say." He flicked a switch, and a voice began. It was deep, grave, adult. "Mr. President, I must direct your attention to a matter of the utmost seriousness. Famine has now reached the following levels—"

Randy cut off the voice, giggling again. "He sounds just like a news announcer."

He punched BREAK and CLS, wiping the screen. Then he pushed RUN and started over, this time in earnest.

Evelyn watched him for a few minutes as he stood, frowning a little, absorbed in the balance he was seeking on the screen. She remembered when school had been like that for her: a challenge and an adventure. She remembered discovering chemistry when she was not much older than Randy. She had loved it even then. How enthralled she had been by the orderly mystery of the world's workings. What a grand kingdom science had seemed to her then; what dreams she had had of the work she would do someday. She had set her heart on being a discoverer, a creator— back when she still thought someone like her could be a real scientist. Watching Randy, her heart ached with pity and loss. Too late, too late, for Randy and for her. A generation ago, she would have been so proud of this boy.

The Augustus, where Evelyn worked evenings, was a small, discreetly inconspicuous restaurant near the Capitol. It was elegantly furnished in dark wood and leather. Evelyn changed into her uniform and began laying out silverware in preparation for the dinner rush. A busboy, passing her, whispered, "Watch out for Jordan; he's in a real mood tonight."

Evelyn nodded. Jordan, the owner, was touchy and harsh with the staff. Perhaps he felt their contempt for one of the bioengineered who had not made anything of himself. But it was undoubtedly because of Jordan that the Augustus had developed its particular clientele.

There was not any one thing to set them apart, yet it was impossible to walk into the restaurant and not recognize that almost everyone there was engineered. Their height was part of it, the healthy vigor and perfect proportions, and the ease of those born to prosperity. Each was striking. Some were the slender, flawless blonds so popular when bioengineering began. But it had not taken long for more exotic looks to catch on. The senator at the table nearest Evelyn was massively built, with a regal African face and blue-black skin. She wondered if his parents were black. The woman across from him looked like an Incan princess, gold jangling from her wrists and ears. In the corner sat a young woman, a federal judge, with the perfect oval face and delicate figure of a woman in a seventeenth-century Chinese painting. Her skin, like that of ladies in such paintings, was dead white.

Evelyn had come to dislike her own face in the mirror. A crowd of norms on the street looked to her like a rough sketch of humanity, with their splotchy complexions and brownish hair, their bodies lumpy, slouched, unfinished. The people in the restaurant were as elegant and vivid as portraits in stained glass.

She went to wait on a man with sand-pale skin and a wiry mane of golden hair. She thought of ancient walls carved with winged lions when she saw his face: beaked nose, deep lines curving down around the full lips, fierce upswept brows. He looked up to give his order, and his eyes were blood-red.

She walked back toward the kitchen, disturbed by those eyes.

They gave him a mad look. There was more and more experimentation going on with appearance, and probably with other things as well. Not everyone would be stopped by the official limits on bioengineering. The engineered were mostly the children of the powerful, and they gathered more power by their own abilities. Where there was power enough, rules would bend.

Waitresses are invisible people. In her work Evelyn heard bits of talk about corporate dealings and government policy centers, universities, publishing, research—all the places where the engineered naturally concentrated. She knew what it meant when a name was mentioned, and someone said, "A five?" and someone else nodded: one of the five percent, one of us.

She and Michael had argued for a long time about engineering their child's appearance. "All this money to engineer high intelligence, good health—I can see that," Michael said. "It's not that important how she looks." Evelyn said, "She has to be recognized as one of them. It'll make a difference in whether she forms the relationships she'll need, whether she really belongs." He shook his head in disapproval and disbelief. "You make it sound like some kind of exclusive club."

"It is!" she said. "The most exclusive club that's ever existed. Members recognize each other instantly, across a room. They give jobs to each other and marry each other and have kids like themselves, or better. The engineered are different from us, Michael. They know it. The difference gets bigger all the time. We can push our daughter across the line before it's too late. . . ."

Evelyn picked up a drink for the red-eyed man, soup for the senator and the princess. She thought of Michael in his production department, supervising other norms. He rarely had direct contact with the engineered writers and editors. Maybe he really did not understand what was happening. Maybe he was too much of an idealist to want to.

But he had to understand. He must not stand in the way of the child.

When she got back to her apartment after work, Michael was stretched out in a chair in the living room, half asleep. He got up to kiss her, and took her raincoat.

"Thanks, dear," she said. "How's Randy?"

"Fast asleep. We almost finished his satellite."

She smiled. "I'm surprised he let you stop at 'almost.' "

She slipped into Randy's room, whispered the light on low, and looked down at him. His dark hair curled over his forehead; his arms were flung above his head in sleep.

When she came back out, Michael had fixed her a drink. While she sat and sipped it, he told her about the new graphics designer at his office. She watched him across the tiny living room: a lanky man with receding hair and a homely, gentle face. She thought, I really am lucky. The five years of their marriage had been hard, with the extra work and constant saving. But Michael had taken it cheerfully. And he was wonderful with Randy.

When she finished her drink, she reached automatically for the shelf near her chair and got out the chart.

Michael shook his head with a touch of exasperation. "Hey—we won't get any farther on that tonight."

"But there are so many decisions to make."

"After we talk to the geneticist. It's nearly midnight, anyway, and we're getting up early. Do you want to be late for your first appointment?"

She thought with a flash of sympathy, he'll be so glad when this is all over and the baby's really on its way. And he was right; she should go to bed. After all the preliminary steps—the Applications Review Board, the interviews with social workers—they had finally been assigned to the geneticist who would do their engineering. They would be meeting the geneticist for the first time in the morning, and she wanted to be fresh for that interview. Still, she couldn't resist opening the chart and running her fingers down it lovingly.

SEX. Female. She had one son. And Michael considered Randy his own, so there was no quarrel.

SOMA-TYPE. Height, build, pigmentation. Hair, skin, eyes. With so many possibilities, how would they ever choose?

INTELLIGENCE. As high as possible, she thought fervently. The highest. So her daughter would never be held back in the work she wanted to do, never meet the helpless, pitying looks of people trying uselessly to explain.

ASSERTIVENESS. There she quarreled with Michael. She wanted high assertiveness—someone who could hold her own. Michael argued for moderation, saying that it made for a happier person. He had teased her gently: "Our daughter doesn't have to be a world-shaker." She had frowned and shaken her head.

SPECIAL TALENTS, RESISTANCES, TOLERANCES . . .

She sighed, laid the chart aside and smiled at Michael. "All right, I'm coming. But *this weekend* . . ."

He threw up his hands in mock dismay. "I concede! This weekend, we'll have it out. Now come on and get some sleep."

It was forty minutes by tubetrain from Washington to New York, half an hour by bus and pedwalk to the towering building that was the East Coast headquarters of the Federal Population and Genetics Commission. They entered from the elevated walkways on the third level and almost immediately got lost. They asked directions twice, wandering through waiting rooms full of plastic benches, past signs that said "GENETICS RATING APPEALS RM 476-A" and "ARTIFICIAL INSEMINATION REGISTRANTS APPLY 1:30–5 PM."

Finally they found the elevators that would take them up to the Genetic Surgery Division. As they waited, it seemed to Evelyn that people glanced at them with a mixture of envy and resentment. Some were probably people with genetic defects, who would not be allowed to have their own children at all. And most people could not afford actual gene surgery, even if they qualified. But we've earned it, Evelyn thought. We've worked long and hard for our chance.

On the twenty-second floor, a receptionist directed them to a small carpeted waiting room. Evelyn sat down and tried to calm herself. After a few minutes a woman walked up to the receptionist's desk. She was remarkably tall, with heavy blond hair pulled into a loose knot at the back of her neck. Her face could only have been created by a Greek sculptor or a bioengineer. She had the classic straight line of forehead and nose, the small bowed mouth, the strong graceful curve from cheek to chin. She beckoned them over and smiled down at them. "I'm Dr. Morland, your geneticist. Please come with me." Her eyes were gray. Of course, Evelyn thought. Gray-eyed Athena, divinely tall . . .

They followed her into a roomy office. Evelyn looked around at the tall windows, the bookshelves, the charts of the double-helix DNA molecule on the wall. Here we are, she thought. It's beginning.

Dr. Morland congratulated them on their decision to have an engineered child. "You two have excellent genetic ratings, and I'm sure that this child will be rewarding both for you and for our society as a whole. Now—since this is your first appointment, let me review the options open to you."

What Morland told them was familiar to Evelyn from Commission publications, until she heard with dismay that prices for most alterations were going up again. She was frantically trying to recalculate costs in her head when Morland reached "intelligence."

"You can choose an IQ range up to approximately one hundred fifty on the Hoffman scale," she said. "That's equivalent to two hundred on the old scale." On the old scale two hundred had been the top, the outer limit. The Hoffman scale just kept going. "The cost for IQ will depend on whether—"

"Excuse me." Evelyn sat up very straight. "I thought that engineering could take the IQ up as high as Hoffman one eighty with no trouble."

Dr. Morland paused. "It can be done, although not without trouble. Nothing involving intelligence is simple. The policy of the Commission is not to aim for more than forty points over the higher of the parents' IQs. Larger gaps tend to produce serious problems in adjustment between parents and child."

"You mean we have no choice? That's a legal limit?"

"It isn't a matter of law. However, it's a firm Commission policy, growing out of our experience. After all, Hoffman one fifty is quite a high IQ."

"But there are already engineered who are higher—and they're having kids now, and their kids can go up another forty points. I don't want my daughter left behind before she even starts."

"Of course not. But that isn't the case." Morland smiled her serene, Greek-goddess smile. "First of all, not all the engineered *want* children brighter than they are. Also, at this point no one can go much beyond one eighty. No single gene controls intelligence. We have to work with a whole series of genes that influence the formation of brain cells, the keenness of certain types of perception, and so on. Those same genes also affect other characteristics, so in trying to increase intelligence, we could produce bad side effects. We don't know enough yet to go too far. Your child will be near the top of the range. She should have every chance to excel in any field she enters."

She paused a moment. Evelyn was sick with resentment.

Morland went on. "The cost of altering intelligence will depend on whether both of you contribute genes. The alternative is to use one gamete from one of you, and the other from an engineered donor who has some of the qualities you want, such as high intelligence. Then we simply have to assure dominance of those qualities by repressing the appropriate genes on your gamete. That's relatively simple. The amount of actual gene surgery —removing some of your genes and inserting others in the chromosomes—is greatly reduced."

She paused, looking from one to the other. Evelyn, her stomach still tight with anger, said nothing.

"We want it to be our own child," Michael said.

Morland nodded. "Many people feel that way."

"It's going to be rough, though," Michael went on. "With these new prices, I'm not sure we can afford all the alterations we had in mind."

She nodded again. "It's too bad, but prices do go up. I see by your preliminary chart that you aren't interested in special tolerances or talents—music and so forth. That's good, since those are quite expensive. As for the rest, you'll have to balance your priorities against what you can afford. I see you have down somatyping, for instance. That's fairly simple, and not so expensive in itself. Still, you might want to save money there and put it toward intelligence."

Michael nodded. "That's probably what we'll have to do. The intelligence is the most important thing, after all."

"That's true. Now—this is the complete schedule of rates. This chart also shows interrelations between various qualities, so you can see the implications of your choices. You'll need to complete these forms. . . ."

Evelyn was staring from Morland to Michael, her face gone rigid. Were they going to pretend that appearance was not important? Michael had promised! She had worked so hard to convince him! And Morland—did she think, because they were norms, it did not matter if their child got second-class treatment?

Michael was on his feet, shaking hands across the desk. "Thank you for your time."

"Certainly. I'll look forward to seeing you again."

Evelyn forced herself to nod and smile politely. Five years, she thought. Scrimping and driving themselves. Now they were trying to steal her daughter's future.

She was silent while they made their way through the huge building to the sunlit plaza. As they walked out, Michael said, "The price rise is a real shame. But now at least we have a better idea just how much we can do."

"You mean how little," Evelyn said.

Michael looked at her, startled. "Hey, come on—it's not that bad."

"It's not? No soma-typing, and limited intelligence—"

"Wait a minute. I wouldn't call Hoffman one fifty limited."

"Oh, it's not—for a norm." Evelyn turned away and walked blindly into the plaza. She stopped before a fountain that sent a dozen jets of water foaming high into the air. All around her, people went briskly about their business, their footsteps clicking on the pavement. Michael came up beside her and took her arm.

"Hon, listen. I know you have your expectations all set—but I think you're overreacting. The doctor's right. She'll still be near the top."

"When the top is already Hoffman one eighty? Do you think thirty IQ points are a slight margin? And the top will keep going up."

"All right. Maybe it will. But you know, there's something to what the geneticist said about the gap between parents and child. I keep thinking of Anna Holden and her son. Remember when he left?"

Anna Holden had lived in their complex for a while: a dowdy, middle-aged woman, pouring her family trust fund into the child of her dreams. She brooded over him constantly, and raged and cried when he went beyond her. "My own son, not even sixteen, and he won't tell me a thing. All day at school, all night in that lab—I'm sorry I had it fixed up for him. He won't even *talk* to me. My own child, my son." What could he say to her? One night she stood screaming down the hall: "Come back here! Come back, you hear me?" Her son strode away, his back straight, his long hair swinging. He had the face of a young Comanche. "I'm your *mother,*" Anna yelled. He paused and turned, giving her a look of measureless contempt. "You?"

Evelyn shook her head, pushing the memory away. "Anna was neurotic—always clinging to him. It's no wonder he wanted to get away." She found herself irrationally angry that Michael had even brought the incident up. She thought, My daughter will never hate me. She calmed herself and went on. "The problem is that you're still thinking in our terms. An IQ of Hoffman one fifty would be outstanding for us. For the engineered, it's only moderate."

"Then moderate may have to do, Evelyn. Do you think we'd be able to fight Commission policy? Do you?"

Evelyn shrugged, not wanting to answer. No, the policy would not yield, not for a couple of norms. She stared at the glittering fountain, and her sense of defeat gradually gave way to a grim determination.

"All right, Michael," she said. "She won't be as smart as some. But she'll be one of the engineered. She'll have a fighting chance to do whatever she wants with her life. We just have to give her what she needs to make the most of her chance. She has to have the soma-typing."

Michael came around in front of her and looked into her eyes. His plain face was intent and troubled. "Listen. I know how you feel about this. And I was willing to go along, before the price rise. But it isn't that important, Evelyn—it just isn't."

She tried to interrupt, but he hurried on. "I want the best for my children—you know that. I want them to have every chance I can give them. I want them to be happy. I want them to contribute something to the world, and take pride in themselves. Those are the things that matter. If she isn't so beautiful that she doesn't even look human, that won't be a tragedy. I'd rather she looked like you."

There was a note of pleading in his voice. He wanted her to yield gracefully, so they would not have to fight—with each other or with circumstances. After their long struggle, he did not want this sourness at the end.

She understood. Sympathy warred with her rising anger, so that her voice came out rough. "Do you think I've waited all these years to have a child who'll be *sort of* engineered? Who'll be on the edges, talked past, ignored? Do you know what it would do to her, to give her engineered intelligence but not make her really one of them? To be held back, looked down on, kept from using what's in her—nothing's worse than that. Nothing could be crueler."

Michael looked away, silenced by her outburst. After a moment he said, "I just don't see how we could do it. With these new prices—I went over our savings just last night. We'll have to take out a loan even without soma-typing. If we want that too, we'd have to work another year, maybe more, and the way the costs keep going up—"

"I'm thirty-six now. We can't afford a host mother. We have to do it soon."

"Well, there you are."

"Oh, no. We'll get a bigger loan."

"What makes you think we can? Our savings will be gone after this, and we won't have much in the way of collateral."

We'll find a bank that'll give us the money, she thought. Or something. Whatever they had to do. There had to be a way.

After a moment of her grim silence, Michael said, "I'm sorry. I know how much this child means to you."

She patted his arm. "It's not your fault." But she rankled inside. It was his child too, wasn't it?

Evelyn was back at the lab by early afternoon. She worked in a rambling, sunny building whose long halls were permeated by a faint medicinal smell compounded of many chemicals. No matter what her mood, entering that building always gave her a secret lift of excitement. The lab was a world leader in biochemical research. That fact still held magic for Evelyn. She worked under Dr. Lin, an engineered biochemist who was designing microorganisms to manufacture cheap, high-quality protein. It was the kind of work Evelyn loved above all others: the merging of discipline and creativity, the reshaping of life itself. She had dreamed of doing that kind of work when she was a student. The engineered had already been moving in everywhere; no one had understood then just what a difference that made.

Evelyn entered Dr. Lin's work area, passed the closed shelves by the door where various cultures were growing and went to the table at the rear of the room. Wilson, on night shift, had been scheduled to set up a Kjeldahl analysis to test the amount of protein in several strains. Evelyn glanced at the flasks on the burner and stopped. "Damn," she said under her breath. She checked each flask. There was no crystallization, nothing to measure. She looked them all over again. Wilson must have left out the catalyst. Of all the stupid times to mess up a routine procedure—She went back to her desk and called Dr. Lin.

Lin came in to look, though there was nothing he could do but fume. Evelyn, checking nutrient levels in the cultures near the lab door, could hear his irritated grumbling. "How could anyone be so careless?"

One of the other researchers had followed him in. He shrugged. "It's bound to happen sometimes. People run these tests over and over, and sometimes they'll slip up."

"Did he have to slip on this one? It'll set back my whole schedule. It'll take two weeks to culture enough of some of these strains for another analysis."

"Well, it's your own fault, really. If it was that important, you shouldn't have left it for the night shift, when the regular supervisors aren't around. You can't leave important work to norms."

There was a split second of realization, of stillness, before Evelyn straightened up and walked away.

Later that afternoon, she worked out a new schedule for comparative protein tests, to cut the time loss as much as possible. Dr. Lin stopped by as she was hanging up her lab coat and getting ready to leave.

"Thanks for doing the new schedule," he said. "If you'd been here, this mistake never would have happened. I don't know what I'd do without you." Seeing the apology in his eyes, she was torn between gratitude and resentment. "You're the best assistant in the whole section," he said. "You're really a very able chemist. If it weren't for bioengineering—"

"I know."

There was a small silence. She smiled stiffly and left.

Evelyn was off work at the restaurant that night, but Michael would be late again. In the living room, after dinner, she called banks. The evening applications clerks regarded her with bland courtesy from the view screen. She had a neat sheet of figures before her in Michael's handwriting; he had done the most recent review of their savings and prospects. She gave the clerks account numbers and balances, income, lists of collateral, credit reference numbers. They punched it all into their terminals, applied their credit equations and politely told her where her upper limit would fall on their standard loan policy charts. Since her loan request was substantially above the limit, they offered her appointments with their loan officers for an individual review of her case. Evelyn set up three appointments. But she knew with a sinking in her stomach that Michael was right. They would not get a loan big enough to cover soma-typing.

She sat with her chin in her hand, thinking. The apartment

was quiet, except for tiny clicks from the dining alcove, where Randy was putting together a puzzle. Where else could she turn? She thought of her sister in Arizona. Evelyn had made her some small loans for graduate school, but they hardly even kept in touch anymore.

"Hey, Mom," Randy called.

"What is it?"

"You want to see my puzzle? I'm almost done."

"Not right now, Randy."

"But I'm almost done, I got it all figured out."

"Not now. I'll look at it later."

"But Mom—"

"Randy," she said sharply, "leave me alone. I'm busy."

He fell silent. She put a hand over her eyes, thinking, What am I going to do? Then she punched call numbers for Arizona. The screen flickered and cleared, and there was her sister, nervous and vaguely apologetic as always. When Evelyn brought up the question of a loan, she looked distressed and began to run on about troubles at the irrigation project. Her designs had been off because of the water needs of the new hybrids, and her supervisor was furious; her husband Warren was facing a shake-up in his department; when the new design programs were installed she might not have a job at all. She really did not see how they could make a loan right then.

Anyway, she added hesitantly, sometimes she wasn't sure that all this engineering was such a good idea after all.

"Oh, come on," Evelyn said, startled into impatience. "Where would we be without it? Who do you think has pulled off most of the breakthroughs of the last twenty years? Industry, transportation, cleaning up the environment, the cities—"

"No more slums in Washington?" her sister asked. Evelyn did not answer. "There are some out here," her sister went on. "And people unemployed—you should see them. What good is an automated factory to the people who used to work there?"

So that's it, Evelyn thought. The human race is remaking itself, and she's worried about losing her job. Aloud, she said, "Things take time. You can't do everything at once."

"No—I know that. It's just that the things that do get done seem to be mostly for the people at the top. And the distance between the top and the bottom just gets bigger. . . ."

Evelyn listened a few minutes longer, then cut the conversation off. She should not have expected her sister to understand, she thought wearily. If she understood, she'd be saving for an engineered child of her own.

Her sister was out and the banks were out. Where else was there, where else . . .

A crash from the kitchen made her jump. "Randy?" she called.

"It's okay, it's not anything," he said. She got up and went to look. Randy was down on his knees, brushing together pieces of the blue-glass serving bowl. He looked up at her, scared.

"Randy! *What* are you doing? You broke our best bowl! You *know* you're not supposed to get into that cupboard."

"I was gonna make something in it. For when Dad gets home —for a surprise." His voice trembled.

"I don't care what you were going to do, you're not allowed— and *stop* that. You'll cut your hands, scraping it up that way. Get me the broom."

He brought the broom and she swept up the pieces. "I'm sorry, Mom," Randy said.

"Well, you ought to be. I don't have time for this kind of thing, Randy. I have things to do."

She knelt and ran her hand over the floor tiles, feeling for any slivers she had missed.

"Are you going to have the new baby soon?" Randy asked in a small voice.

"As soon as we can manage," Evelyn said irritably.

"Cost a lot of money to have an engineered baby, doesn't it?"

"It certainly does."

"Is it really exciting?"

Evelyn looked up. Randy was plucking studiously at a towel that hung by the sink. Children, she thought. The times they pick to need reassurance.

"Come over here, Randy," she said. Still kneeling, she put her arm around his waist as he came up. His eyes were large and brown—so like her own. "Sure, it's exciting. But norm babies are too. Having an engineered baby is a good thing to do, because people like that can help us solve a lot of the world's problems. Raising a baby is a lot of work, though. We'll need you to help us."

"Won't she be smarter than me and everything?"

"Someday she will. For a long time she'll be your little sister, and you'll have to help her. Someday she'll be smarter than all of us. But she'll still be ours."

When she had put Randy to bed, she came back to sit in the living room and think about money. She did not know where to turn. The tiny apartment, the crampedness that had never bothered her before, seemed to close in on her. She felt trapped and alone. Michael was tired, and he did not understand, and he was not going to try anymore. Even if she found someplace to borrow the money, she would have to convince him all over again that soma-typing mattered. She rubbed at her eyes in weary frustration. This child was the most important event in her life, but the decisions were still half his, and he could block her. In a flash of anger she thought, I ought to just leave. Then I could make my own choices.

She was shocked by the thought. Leave Michael? After five years of happy marriage? Besides, added a coolly rational part of her mind, if she left she would lose half the savings. She would never be able to pay for the surgery.

She stood up abruptly. Nonsense, nonsense. Michael was a good, kind man. Somehow they would work this all out.

The next morning was Saturday. Michael, with Randy helping, began cooking chicken and chopping vegetables for the next week's meals. Evelyn could hear them talking in the kitchen while she spread out the family financial records on the desk in the bedroom. She did not doubt that Michael had been thorough, but in her restlessness she had to see for herself. She began going over Michael's figures, checking the price increases against their savings and projected incomes.

Half an hour later, she called Michael. Her voice was strained. He came to the bedroom door, a paring knife in his hand, Randy close behind. "What is it, hon?"

"Michael, we have six thousand dollars more in savings than you put down here."

He stared at her blankly for a few seconds. Then he frowned. "You know what that's for."

"We can replace it later," she said, her voice rising. "We need it now. What are you trying to do?"

Michael touched Randy's shoulder. "You go on and finish peeling the potatoes. Be careful with the knife, like I showed you. Your mother and I have to talk." Randy looked from one to the other. Then he left.

Michael closed the door. He came over to the side of the bed near the desk and slowly sat down. "We're going to have a second child," he said. "But we already have one. No matter what we've done without, we've always put a little something aside for Randy's education, so he would have that much security. That isn't going to change now."

"*You're* telling *me* that? You've decided what my son needs, and you weren't even going to discuss it with me?"

Michael's face darkened. "He's my son too."

"Oh, I know you love Randy. That's not the point. He won't need the money for years, and by then we can replace it."

"We shouldn't be replacing it. We should be adding to it. It's not going to be much in any event, with costs the way they are. We won't be able to add much after the girl is born, with all the tests and psychologists and special schools—"

"So you just decided, you just decided all by yourself—"

Evelyn's voice was rising, but Michael shouted over her. "What do you mean, I decided? It never occurred to me you'd want to use Randy's money."

"It's too late for Randy. Whatever it costs, we have to make this child—"

"Right, right. We have to make her one of the masters of the earth." He waved his hand in dismissal, but she flared back at him.

"You say that and you think it's just an expression. But it's real. They *are* the masters of the earth—the new human beings. Can't you understand that? Whatever's worth running, they run —politics, business, education—"

"Is that all that matters to you? Randy's a person too. We can't take everything away from him—"

"Then we'll use a donor. If we use an engineered donor's genes instead of yours, it'll be cheaper, and we can afford everything."

"Instead of *my* genes? When you've already had a child, and I haven't? Oh, no. How about using a donor instead of *your* genes?"

"No. No."

"Why not? The child would still be yours, more than Randy is mine—out of your own body, and with you from birth."

"No." Evelyn shook her head slowly back and forth. "I have to have my daughter."

Michael laughed with a bitterness that shocked her. "Of course. You have to have *your* daughter. The new you that can do all the things you can't. Do you really think you can live through a child?"

Evelyn's face went cold. When she answered, her voice shook. "I don't care what you say. She's going to have the chance I didn't. And she'll be my daughter."

"Mine too, believe me. So—no donors."

"Then we'll have to use Randy's money."

"No."

Evelyn closed her hands and eyes tightly for a moment, then tried once more.

"Michael, listen. Randy is my son, my first child. He'll always be special to me, even more just because he *is* a norm, because he's like us. But we can't afford to pretend. He's *only a norm.*"

Michael stared. "So anything this other child needs—pretty hair, anything—is more important than Randy."

"She is! She's more important than any of us."

"My God, Evelyn. What are you saying? A family can't live

that way. If that's the way it's going to be, I don't want an engineered child at all!"

"Then don't have one!" She jumped to her feet. "You don't deserve one!" He was just like all the other sheep. What had ever made her think she wanted his genes in a child of hers?

But Michael's anger suddenly dissolved, and he sat shaking his head. "Evelyn, Evelyn, look what's happening. We've waited for this for so long. We can't let it set us against each other."

She watched his homely face, twisted with concern, and felt a flood of contempt. It was the same contempt she felt for her own face in the mirror. Weak, she thought. The engineered are right to look down on people like him.

Michael came toward her, fumbling for her hands. "I don't want to fight with you."

Evelyn did not meet his eyes. A thought had occurred to her, simple and cool as first light. She could get most of the savings from him in exchange for custody of Randy.

Again she recoiled from her own thoughts, shocked and ashamed. To give up Randy, to *sell* him—Still, the small cool thoughts unfolded. She could afford it then—her child, using her genes and sperm from a donor. It would be cheaper. And better.

"We can work it out," Michael was saying. "We're both upset right now, that's all. I didn't mean to deceive you about Randy's money, I really didn't."

"I know," she said. "We're both tired." Never to see Randy again. Oh, the stab of loss at the thought. And yet, underneath, so deep she could almost ignore it, there ran a treacherous current of relief. Never again to be wrenched by pity and regret. No more to see his face, the mirror of her own: her own failure comfirmed in the eyes of her son.

Michael's hands were warm and tight around hers. He was her husband; he was a good man. Once more he said, "We'll work it all out."

She tried to smile. Still, she did not meet his eyes. "Of course we will," she said. But she knew already that they would not work it out.

NOTES ON CONTRIBUTORS

LUCIUS SHEPARD was born in Lynchburg, Virginia, "raised hell in high school and hallucinated for a year and a half at the University of North Carolina." He has been, among other things, a rock musician, a bouncer in a Spanish whorehouse (the Club Amigo in Málaga) and a steerer for a perfume merchant named Abdul Affifi in the Khan al Khalili bazaar of Cairo. He has sold two novels since attending Clarion in 1980. The first, *Green Eyes*, will have appeared by the time you read this.

KRISTI OLESEN grew up in Milwaukee and left it at fifteen to attend an experimental high school in Oslo, Norway. Since then she has spent most of her time in San Francisco. She is involved in theater production and has spent two seasons as a dresser at the American Conservatory Theatre.

NINA KIRIKI HOFFMAN was born in San Gabriel, California, and attended Santa Barbara City College. In 1977 she moved to Moscow, Idaho, which, for some reason, is a hotbed of writers.

DEAN WESLEY SMITH, who lives in Moscow, Idaho, and is a friend of Nina Hoffman's, was born in Boise, took a degree in architecture at the University of Idaho and spent two years in law school. He has been a professional golfer, a ski instructor, bartender, disc jockey, school-bus driver, etc. He owns a bookstore in Moscow.

"JAN HERSCHEL" is the pseudonym of a writer who was born in Adelaide, South Australia, and "spent a long time at Flinders University studying Anglo-Saxon, Old Norse, Middle English and the works of Marshall McLuhan."

PATRICIA LINEHAN is a dog breeder and has written about dogs for *The Windhound, Dog World,* and *The AKC Gazette.*

GARY W. SHOCKLEY, who was Lucius Shepard's suitemate at Clarion, was born in Fort Wayne, Indiana. He is now a computer programmer at Control Data Corporation in Sunnyvale, California.

WILLIAM KNUTTEL was born in Philadelphia and now lives in the Bay Area of California, where he works as a winemaker and plays go.

MARIO MILOSEVIC was born in Cava de' Tirreni, Italy, of Yugoslavian parents who were on their way to North America. He spent the first year of his life in an Italian refugee camp. Milosevic and his wife, Kim Antieau, met at Clarion in 1980. They live in Bandon, Oregon.

BARBARA RAUSCH was born in Indianapolis and spent most of her early life in Michigan, where she taught elementary art in the Flint public schools for seventeen years. In 1982 she moved to Los Angeles to pursue a career as a cartoonist.

MCNEVIN HAYES grew up in Detroit; he now lives with another Clarionite, Fax Goodlife, in the woods near Cheshire, Oregon. He has been an assistant film director, vacuum cleaner salesman, waiter, bookstore clerk, etc.

RENA LEITH was born in Evanston, Illinois, and earned a B.A. in technical communications from Purdue. She turned down the only job offer she got in her field, from Lawrence Livermore Laboratories, because she was morally opposed to the work they were doing. She has been a photographic retoucher, a field laborer, a drugstore clerk; at one time she was head cashier of the Fort Wayne, Indiana, office of Merrill Lynch, Pierce, Fenner & Smith. She now lives in Austin, Texas.

LOIS WICKSTROM was born in Boston and has a degree in biology put together from coursework in five universities. She is the editor and publisher of *Pandora*.

RENA YOUNT was one of the founders of a radical/antiwar paper in the early seventies; after that she spent four years with Source, a collective that published books for community organizers. She has been a waitress, a secretary, a graphic designer, a newsletter editor and (currently) a data librarian.

DAMON KNIGHT—as an editor, a short story writer, and a critic—has been an influential force in the science fiction field for over thirty years. He was the founder and first president of Science Fiction Writers of America, and the co-founder of the first workshop for science fiction writers, the Milford Science Fiction Writers' Conference. As an anthologist, he is perhaps best known for the acclaimed *Orbit* series, in which many award-winning stories of the sixties and seventies were published for the first time. His most recent novel is *The Man in the Tree*. He and his wife, the writer Kate Wilhelm, have taught at Clarion for many years.